THE DIAMOND COLLECTION

by

Michael James Cook

THE DIAMOND COLLECTION - ISBN 9798449973733

Writer and Author is Mr Michael James Cook
Designed by Virtual Admin UK - www.virtualadminuk.co.uk
Printed by Amazon

THE

DIAMOND

COLLECTION

DEDICATION

This book is dedicated to all those who devote their lives to caring for and meeting the needs of others.

ABOUT THE AUTHOR

Michael James Cook was born in North Reddish, Stockport, Cheshire in 1942 and was educated at Stockport School (Grammar) and the universities of Durham, Bristol and Exeter. A promising career in professional sport was dashed at an early age by a serious knee injury. He was an ordinand of the Church of England and a full-time Youth Leader in Bristol. He was one of the first full-time Teacher/Youth Leaders to be appointed in Cheshire. He taught for 30 years in Secondary Modern, Comprehensive and Grammar schools in Cheshire, Devon, Durham, Essex and Somerset before taking early retirement due to ill-health. As a young man, he took the F.A. Coaching course and was for many years a part-time scout for a number of Football League clubs; soccer remaining the first love of his life. He is a published author, poet, songwriter and photographer.

"A poet looks at the world the way a man looks at a woman."
Wallace Stevens

"Poetry is the rhythmical creation of beauty in words."
Edgar Allan Poe

CONTENTS

Foreword

FOREWORD

My wife Marjorie and I have selected these poems to celebrate our sixty years of married life together, as well as my eightieth birthday.

Ours was a love story like no other. We met at Scarborough in the summer of 1959 when she was fifteen and I was seventeen. We were there on holiday. Neither of us had been there before. On the Sunday evening after we each arrived, we met by chance while taking an evening stroll with friends through the Italian Gardens. After that, we saw each other as much as possible during the remaining week. Our final meeting was at The Mere on the Friday, where I asked her to marry me and she said "Yes". As I didn't have a ring, I tied a long blade of grass round the fourth finger of her left hand.

We were both still at grammar school; me in my home town of Stockport and she in Newcastle Upon Tyne. After we returned home, we wrote to each other virtually every day for that first year and saw each other whenever we could during the school holidays, taking it in turns to stay at each other's homes. I managed to gain a place at Durham University for the following year.

When I arrived home after we met, I wrote my first ever poem and sent it to Marjorie. It was entitled Alone Reflecting In The Sun. My second one was When You Are Bored which I wrote inside her Rutherford High School copy of Twelfth Night, which she still has today.

I was never an academic pupil. My only incentive to attend school was the sport. English was my worst subject and I even failed English Language at GCE 'O' level and had to retake it in the November before they would admit me into the Sixth Form (as it was then) to do my 'A' levels. By this time a promising professional career in sport had been put in doubt by a serious knee injury with specialists telling me I would never play again.

At University I concentrated on my academic studies catching up on lost time. My first book was published when I was nineteen years old and only then did I begin to realise my full potential. I became a teacher. The rest, as they say, is history…..

Michael James Cook

<u>INTRO</u>

ON THE SHELF

If you should see me on a shelf
Looking lost, all by myself,
Please pick me up and take a look,
I'm not like any other book.

Inside you'll find the reason why
I can make you laugh or cry;
Be your friend for many a day,
Either at work or when you play.

I'm full of verses penned with care,
Poetic thoughts I'll gladly share,
So don't pass by without a glance,
Some loves are born as if by chance.

AT FIRST SIGHT

That first glance,
That first spark,
That surge of pure elation;
Desirous to possess such beauty,
Such perfection in another.
Like a miracle of Nature,
Difficult to comprehend,
Or reason How? Or Why?
The welcome in your eyes,
Your luscious lips
Which softly mouth "Come in",
Invite a confident response,
Positively charged.
Then to find our bodies faultless fit
To form a channel
For our unadulterated lust
Through which great tidal waves
Of passion roar
Like the Severn river's bore.
To fall in love, so commonplace,
Requires a special time,
A unique face,
For that first glance
And that first spark
Which quickens the heart.

Gradually, over time we learn
That falling out of love, in turn,
Is just as easy.
For relationships to last
We need to study what has passed.
Love is neither falling in nor out,
But 'doing' is what it's all about.
Commitment is an act of will.
Caring, a duty to fulfil.
Immature, our "love" is wild,
And lust alone is not enough
To raise a child.

COME TOGETHER

Meeting you
Wanting you
Lustful sighs.
Chance a miss,
Steal a kiss
Catch your eye.
Sex invites
Age divides,
Love provides.
Snap greetings
Hopes leaping,
Sad "goodbyes".
Bright flowers
Lonely hours
Passing by.
Hidden notions
Blocked emotions,
Wondering why.
Words deceiving
Off-hand dealings,
Compounded lies.
Actions adding
Guilt subtracting,
Passion multiplied.
Emotional pain
Conflicting aims,
Needs compromised.
Purple patches
Golden fractures
In a winter's sky.

Days of pleasure,
Gifts to treasure,
Money can't buy.
Poetic Rhymes
Romantic times
Which fate supplies.
Flesh embracing,
Faith performing
Miracles inside.
Senses blooding,
Urges flooding,
Ecstatic sighs.
The devil's dam
Tempted Adam
Innocence died.
The laws of men
The censor's pen
Stems not the tide.
In vacant space
There is a place
Where lust abides.
Mother Nature
Orders reason
To stand aside.
So come, let's fly
Across an unknown sky
To a life we cannot deny.

MYSELF

I'm inclined to be good and inclined to be bad.
I'm usually happy but sometimes I'm sad.
I try to do good but so often I fail.
I'm undoubtedly witty, but my wit can grow stale.

Some call me a fool, others say that I'm wise.
I'm probably both but they don't realise
The fact that we're all a little of each.
Perfection is something quite out of our reach.

They say I'm eccentric, it's true I can tell.
One moment in heaven, the next I'm in hell.
I tend to be cautious and common with sense.
I'm very understanding, but sometimes I'm dense.

Occasionally, I'm stupid and very unwise.
I'm usually honest but I sometimes tell lies.
I'm very observant and seldom forget.
The moments of pleasure with people I've met.

I'm extremely obliging, respectful and kind.
I never shoot dogs nor people who are blind.
I'm very considerate as you can well see.
Although I forget things, I've a good memory.

Independent, yet faithful, and loyal till the end,
I'm a perfect companion to stranger or friend.
Yet proud and conceited, I'm humble and low,
Sarcastic and lazy, untidy and slow.

I'm a likeable person as everyone knows;
Me, most of all, as each moment it grows -
My liking myself that little bit more -
Good on the surface but bad to the core.

Footnote: Written in the library of Stockport School during a study period when I was in the 6th Form.

FOR YOU MY LOVE

For you my love, words from my pen will flow for ever,
Scribing time-eternal thoughts which may seem clever.
Come to my side and sit with me, fair maiden still.
You are my hope, for helpless is my will.
There is a reason for the twisted tortured way I feel;
I'm just a dreamer, I cannot comprehend what's real.
There is but one journey's end to each upon the earth;
Our bodies are a-dying from the moment of our birth.
So when the testing comes, I'll stay your fears,
Stand firm throughout and shed no mournful tears.
And when the raging storm has passed you by,
If you should turn and chance your eye,
You'll find me standing by your side,
For love-found moments never die.

Footnote: Written at my parent's bungalow in Weston-Super-Mare in a letter to my wife in Stockport during the time I had a temporary teaching post at Weston Boys Grammar School, before taking up my permanent post at Axminster School in the September as Head of Religious and Social Education.

I'LL DO ANYTHING

Throw me a rubber and I'll rub out my name.
Give me a gun and I'll blow out my brains.
Show me the sun and I'll hold back the rain.
Love me today and I'll love you the same.
Leave me tomorrow and I'd die from the pain.
Do what you like I'll take all the blame.
Deceive me, desert me, I'll cover your shame.
Reject me, forsake me, I'll forgive you again.
Ignore me, forget me, my love will remain.

HAPPY ANNIVERSARY

I could wax lyrical with exaggerated ease
Describing our past six decades shared.
Though my words would surely easily please
They could not justify how much we've cared.

The day we met, which changed our lives for good,
Lives long in the mind where memories hide.
A chance encounter in the twinkling of an eye we stood
In a garden of Eden, where lovers' paths collide.

Whose was the hand which guided both our steps?
What arrows of desire triggered our transformation?
Mesmerised, we tasted love, its whims and depths.
Virgin kisses sealed our quest for further exploration.

Enforced partings and separations obstructed our way,
Knots of emotion bound us ever closer together.
Love letters writ and posted each passing day,
Containing our hopes and dreams, whatever the weather.

Outside the church, camera flash bulbs shed some light,
All shrouded in mist like the fog on the Tyne,
You posed on that freezing winter's day, turned night,
My Geordie angel so bright and sublime.

We tied the bonds and vowed we'd never fall.
We tried to overcome the wrongs which God forbids.
We toiled to do our best for one and all,
To make the world a better place by what we did.

As years passed by and long days became short,
We entered the Twilight Zone with fading sight.
The sword of Damocles, an ever-present thought;
Uncertainty and dread with sleepless nights.

Tiredness has become our daily cloak and shroud,
While seasons and festivals slowly lose their shine.
Peace is all we seek when others grow too loud.
In truth, our love is stronger now than in its prime;
A life-line, certain to serve us both a lifetime.

GUEST REQUESTS

FOR

Tricia Jardine - Alone Reflecting In The Sun

Paddy Martin - At The Silver Blades Ice Rink

Josie Gatley - Chard Sunset

Dorothy Bambridge - Come The Spring

Joan Wedgwood - Happiness

Thelma Clarke - Knitting

Derek English - Lunar Eclipse

Ken Bamford - New Hope

John Hind - Ode To A Cook

Patricia Martin - Stars

Suzanne Bamford - The Potter

Bob Wain - Views Around Kynance

ALONE, REFLECTING IN THE SUN

If you could only be with me this moment and the more
To share this peaceful hour but for a little while.
To stop and rest and think; it is worthwhile.
To reflect, to recollect, and then to pass a smile....
Some things well remembered and others best forgot:
The things we ought to do, the things we ought not.
To think a little time of nature and of life,
And the reason and the purpose we participate in strife.
Each day we live to encounter good and bad;
Some things make us happy and others make us sad.
Is this for nought or is there sense in all?
Is there an end and does man live to fall?
Each individual, born to make the choice between
Belief, or disbelief, as it may seem
To him or her who thinks of these and other things,
From whence our hearts be heavy or may sing.
And when we die, what then; are we but waste?
All knowledge stored in life to rot in but a buried place?
No use, no aim, no after-death, no life to come?
We are alive this peaceful hour,
Alone, reflecting in the sun.

Footnote: Written while sunbathing in the garden at home in South Reddish, Stockport after returning from a holiday in Scarborough where I met Marjorie. This was the first poem I ever wrote and I wrote it for her.

AT THE SILVER BLADES ICE-RINK

Swirling figures in cold air
Sliding and gliding
Gracefully
Over the crispy surface
Of the hard ice.

Packs of people pick their way
Stumbling and tumbling
Seemingly
In a frenzied trance-like dance
Anti-clockwise.

Steel silver blades underfoot
Hissing and swishing
Constantly
Cutting round the glassy rink
Menacingly.

Occasional spills of blood
Slipping and tipping
Carelessly
With splinters of brittle bone
Cracked on impact.

Footnote: Written on the coach returning to Axminster School after an end of term outing (for 14 year olds) to the ice rink in Bristol.

CHARD SUNSET

Glorious glow of the descending sun
With golden puffs floating across
The darkening sky.
Smoke from a garden bonfire hangs
Suspended in a leaning spiral
Tapering to a tip.
Silver bird with vapour trail
Silently sweeps across the copper hue,
Painting an ormolu streak,
Which runs unblended on the horizon.

High above the town
Trees stand to attention, like sentries,
Silhouetted against the sunset,
Guarding the ridge to Snowdon Hill.

To the east, the heavens already sparkle;
Blue-black velvet spangled with stars,
Dressed for night, by a wave
From Tinkerbell's magic wand.
Beneath, in Cathedral silence,
Lies the town in a crystal bowl;
A study of still life,
Lit by the embers of a dying fire.

Footnote: First published in the Axminster News on 17.06.1976, the poem is a description of the view from the back of our house in Nursery Gardens, Chard, where we lived for 17 years.

COME THE SPRING

Come the spring when maidens sing,
Come the day when winter has gone.
Then we'll hear the bluebells ring
And the birds mating songs.
Come the time when young men sow,
Seeds of love since times long ago,
Then we'll see every newborn,
Come the spring.

Come the spring we'll dance and sing,
Work and play to nature in song;
She will wear golden rings
In her hair all day long.
Come the night and shady moon,
Casting spells with magical tunes,
Then we'll hear every newborn,
Come the spring.

Come the wind to have its fling,
Come the rain when days are not long,
Dawns of dew, clear skies bring,
Leaves of green growing strong.
Come the sun and rainbows bright,
Linking Earth with Heaven's delight,
Then we'll greet every newborn,
Come the spring.

HAPPINESS

Happiness is like an elusive shadow,
Needing contrast, dark and light,
To give it form
And people to make it viable.

Happiness can be bought.
Like an unwilling slave,
It will work for a while
Then disappear with
Diminishing appreciation;
Desire having secured the escape
By loosening the chains of bondage.

Happiness can be taught
By punishment and reward
In the school of ambition.
Motivated by discontent
It becomes an ideal;
An aim to be realised
Through suffering and deprivation.

Happiness can be sought,
But to seek we first
Must discover the clue
To its ultimate source.
The more we look
The less we'll be satisfied.
For we cannot find it - it finds us.

Happiness can be caught.
It is infectious and spreads
With our caring and sharing.
We cannot contain it,
We cannot retain it.
We receive more if we pass it on,
For happiness is essentially free.

KNITTING

Click-click; click-click,
Go the knitting needles
As the old grey-haired woman
Rocks in her rocking chair
To and fro.
On the wall
The clock goes
Tick-tock, tick-tock,
As she knits.
Her mind wanders
As her hands draw
Semi-circles with the wool;
Up and down,
Backwards and forwards.
She is lost in the past;
Memories making
Patterns in her head.
She dreams of the future
Hoping all her plans
Will materialise,
Like the cardigan
She is knitting.
Click-click; click-click.
And time ticks by
As the clock
On the wall
Goes tick-tock, tick-tock.

Footnote: _One of three poems written on the same day; the others being 'Little Children' and 'Colour TV'. The image is one of my wife's mother knitting while seated in our rocking chair, where I had written the two poems previously._

LUNAR ECLIPSE

As the sun sinks in the West,
Makes me think of home,
Where all the folk are resting
Till the coming of the dawn.

And slowly as the sun sets
I'm drawn to reminisce,
Thinking of my loved one -
It's her the most I miss.

The colours gently darken
And shadows lengthen more,
I reach out in the darkness
To what we had before.

The rising moon gives lovers
On half the Earth alone,
Hopes to be united
In "heavens" of their own.

NEW HOPE

Hope has a new dawn every day;
The sound of singing far away,
A footprint in the desert sand,
Smiles from a stranger in a foreign land.

Hope has new horizon faces
Lighting up the darkest places.
Like a traveller through time,
Hope is a servant of mankind.

Hope is the offspring we require
Born to the helpless to inspire,
Child of the embers of desire,
Raised like a Phoenix from a fire.

Hope has all the saving graces,
Kicking over all the traces.
When we encounter testing storms
Hope is a coat to keep us warm.

A coin cast in a wishing well,
Messaged bottle on ocean's swell,
When we have faith enough to float
Hope will arrive to help us cope.

On stormy seas of black despair,
Come guiding hands from those who care.
The Promised Land of every prayer;
God's lifeboat fit to take us there.

ODE TO A COOK

The chef stood on the flaming deck
Feeling hot and flustered.
The galley fire consumed the ship
Because he'd burnt the custard.

STARS

Stars are suns in the night.
Some are dead and some are bright.
They twinkle in the sky and give it light.
They offer hope of other forms of life.

The stars are company to our own,
In a universe which is our home,
Where one day man might freely roam.
Without them we'd be lonely and alone.

In billions of years our sun will die,
The human race will have to fly;
If all our hopes are to survive,
We need those suns to keep us starry-eyed.

Footnote: Written in the evening of the same day as the poem 'Questions About Life' after a discussion about astronomy.

23

THE POTTER

The potter's wheel spins;
The potter in control
Moulds the clay
Gently with his hands
Giving form to shapes
Within his mind.

His mind, his hands, his wheel,
Work in unison,
In concentrated effort,
Developing skills to create
Precision and perfection
Out of nothing.

The potter is a useful being;
He helps us to see ourselves.
We too could imitate the potter
In motive, effort and deed;
Not making pots, but peace
And order out of chaos.

Footnote: Written on the same day as 'Lost Love' and 'Heavy Shower' while attending evening classes in pottery at Holyroad School, Chard.

VIEWS AROUND KYNANCE

Westward on the distant horizon line
Rests Penwith, now glass clear, now smudged in haze;
A granite peninsula, dark, remote,
Like a watching finger marking time.
Across Mounts Bay, flash red and white rays;
The eyes of Wolf Rock searching out boats
Around Land's End, down a coast of serpentine.

Behold! Kynance, showplace of the Lizard,
With its manifold elaborations;
The Gull Rock and Asparagus Island;
Black rocks colour-washed like witch and wizard;
A cove, steeple pierced with incantations,
Rainbows of spray above floss-silk sand.
It's beauty fretted by winter blizzards.

Behind, bulked large, the headland of the Rill:
A tableland's edge, whence first was sighted
The coming of the Spanish Armada.
Before, sits Lion Rock, with looks to kill,
Guarding the cove and cliffs, his mane blighted,
Head turned, watching the sea and its saga
Beneath the ridge of Yellow Carn, quite still.

Inland, to the north, are the war-stained downs,
Where airfields scar and slice both hill and heath.
Predannack, Goonhilly and far Culdrose
With tumuli and furze in stoney ground;
Land most holy, enchanted, wild and bleak
Now house a heliport, saucers and roads;
Solitude shed by the droning of sound.

East of the Lion, the scarf of Pentreath,
A sweep of sand against fierce cliffs' wall,
Brushed by the foaming surf of man-high waves.
Yet Pentreath is a plain and tranquil beach,
The most romantic and charming of all,
Where adders bask on hot summer days
And men go a'launcing on moonlit trysts.

Below our window, the end of the lawn,
Where cropped grass topples into barley fields
Which slope to the sea to the south and west.
From here we see vessels Atlantic born
And pass away as the sea-sky yields.
Of all panoramas this is the best;
Large ships and small boats parading from dawn.

Southward, the land falls to old Lizard Head
And a vast arc of luminous green sea.
Beyond are The Stags and old Man o' War;
Great stones out of sight, dark reefs for the dead.
Rocks to which only shags and cormorants flee.
A coastguard lookout hut above the shore
Acts as medic to a constant deathbed.

A little below us along the road
Beside Maenheere where a Tricolour waved,
On the first morning of Armistice Day,
A Belgian widow and daughter abode.
The husband drowned but his parrot was saved;
Some say the shock made the parrot turn grey.
What happened to them is no longer told.

Down farther yet to narrow Rocky Lane,
Sunk between bramble, boulder and high fern;
And on, beside squelching trickle of stream
To Pistol Meadow, of mounded square fame,
Where two hundred souls, from legend we learn,
Were washed ashore and then buried in seams;
Men of war felled by the Rock of that name.

It is said hordes of dogs raced to the scene
To eat the bodies cast up from the wreck.
Hundreds of firearms and cannon were found
But wreckers soon came to pick the place clean.
Don't go at night if you value your neck.
It is haunted and eerie, odd without sound,
And many strange sights are said to be seen.

Cross over the stream where tamarisks hang.
Step up the steep weedy stairs to the cliff
Which leads to the least troubled Lizard cove.
Behind us the seaweed camomile tang.
Ahead, the old lifeboat station and slip,
Polpeor, where Tennyson bathed, I'm told,
And on to the southernmost point of land.

About us, a chain of bright brimming pools,
The spatter of pebbles and sand on shore,
The incessant wash and drag of the tide,
A natural arch, a cavern for fools.
Gullies, clefts, coves, caves and rock-falls galore;
A coastline dragon-green monster waves ride
Breathing white fire, crested with silver, they rule.

Eastward, the lighthouse lime washed dazzling white,
Directs the liners, oil-tankers and boats
Away from the booming cannon-fired sea.
Its beam like a tongue, licks the skyline night,
Silently warning anything afloat
Of treachery beneath, on bended knee;
The beam like a sword at the Old Head swipes.

Return along lanes meandering back
Past Penmenner House, now only a wraith,
Down an arras of fuchsia draping stone,
Where wallflowers roof the rough gravel track
Beyond feathered plumes of tamarisk waifs
To the house "Kynance Bay", once Trewin's home.
Views around here the rest of Cornwall lacks.

Footnote: Written in Room 3 of the Kynance Bay Hotel which my wife and I occupied during the heatwave of August 1976. Each stanza consists of seven decasyllabic lines rhyming abcabca.

SOME VERSE FORMS

A BALLADE OF THE SEA

Paragon of power, the pundits say,
Your breathing causes waves to rise and fall.
Bathers run to greet you shouting "Hurray"
But your swift embrace can become a maul
And the kiss of death awaits one and all.
Your beauty is deceptive; blue is grey.
Standard colours of tyrants always pall;
You will not have your way with me today.

Tempestuous lover enticing and gay,
Luring your victims from behind your shawl,
Leading both young and old alike astray.
There are suckers at every market stall
And you, old-timer with your loathsome gall
Give licence to travel and right of way
To any who ask it, both great and small.
You will not have your way with me today.

There is nothing for which we do not pay.
You foam at the mouth when angry in squall
And your frothy tongue licks round every bay.
Hard rugged rocks and coastlines form a wall,
Hence to be washed away, however tall.
Ships, homes, lives of people at work or play.
But I am not to be part of your haul,
You will not have your way with me today.

Envoi

Sea, I can hear your terrible hunger call;
The rumblings in your belly as you sway.
Yes, even I can touch you when you crawl.
You will not have your way with me today.

Footnote: Also written in Room 3 of the Kynance Bay Hotel on The Lizard. The last stanza, headed Envoi opens with the name of the subject to whom the poem is addressed and sums up the tenor of the whole. The last line is the same in all stanzas. The rhyme scheme is ababbcbc x 3 + bcbc.

A SONNET TO ADAM

Before shadowy dawn I made a vow
To pay the debts of time, and needs repair.
Alone, I heard my lies denote despair;
Today, the voice of conscience takes a bow.
The stage is set to make amends from now
And players all assembled more aware,
Prepare the scene to end a Grande Affaire.
Insight: a curtain, slowly drawn somehow;
I touch your arm, an old reminder sign,
To draw attention more to what's in hand.
I must confess a frailty found in Man;
As Eve in Eden once betrayed her line,
The Fall is played again in every land.
Enjoy the fruits of love as best you can.

Footnote: An example of a fourteen-line sonnet of iambic pentameters consisting of two parts, the octet and sestet in the usual Petrarchan form rhyming abbaabba – cdecde. There are other forms like the Shakespearean (ababcdcd – efefgg) and the Miltonic (abbaabba – cdcdcd).

ASPIRING POET

Michael James Cook
Set out to write a poetry book.
As words flowed from verse to verse
His poems grew steadily worse.

Footnote: The poem is an example of a Clerihew which is a four lined poem rhyming aabb. It is supposed to begin with the name of the person to be discussed or described. It was invented by Edmund Clerihew Bentley. The lines must be of unequal syllabic length and the result is intended to be risible.

AT SEAHOUSES

Seahouses, grey and so damp did seem
And dark were the islands of Farne.
The waves lay calm but the seagulls screamed
And still was the air with alarm.

The morning mist o'er the sea did rise
And pale shone the watery sun.
The time had come for the seals to die
And cold were the hearts of our young.

The fishermen in their boats stood proud
But sad were the eyes of my son.
Policemen came to control the crowds
Who cried that the deed be not done.

Then the marksmen with their guns held tight
Went out on the ebb of the tide.
Their shots rang out and the seals took fright,
For them there was no place to hide.

Three thousand seals, grey and white, lay dead
And gone was their watery calm.
Their blood flowed quick and the sea turned red
And black were the clouds over Farne.

*Footnote: Written in Ballad stanza form, with quatrains
rhyming abab etc. Written during a stay at the Bamburgh
Castle Hotel, Seahouses, at the time of the seal cull,
Easter 1975.*

A WRITTEN PROPOSAL

Shy thoughts on paper surface dwelling,
One probing pen to poke them into life.
Wild words can do their business stirring strife,
Making yet breaking tension; doubts dispelling.

A rush of tears to eyelids welling;
A careless phrase may cut us like a knife.
Shy thoughts on surface paper dwelling;
One probing pen to poke them into life.

In a world where literacy is selling
And the use of written words is rife,
Dare I take the plunge and beg you be my wife?
Shy thoughts on surface paper dwelling;
One probing pen to poke them into life.

*Footnote: This is an example of a Rondel consisting of 13
lines in 3 stanzas rhyming abba, abab, abbab. The first two
lines of the poem are also the last two lines of both the
second and third stanzas.*

BEYOND OUR KEN (HAIKU)

Things exist which we
Don't hear, see, smell, taste or touch;
Our sixth sense says so.

Footnote: This is an example of a Haiku. A Haiku is a Japanese form of poetry expressing a single idea, consisting of 3 lines of 5-7-5 syllables. It does not rhyme or have any metrical regularity.

BLOW IT

No fun to be abed
To doze and fry
With raging head.

No fun to wake and sigh
As those not home
Leave you to die.

No fun to ache alone
At war with germs
Inside your bones

No fun when eyelids burn
And others gloat
It's now your turn.

No fun a red raw throat
Hot steaming nose
Slit eyes afloat.

Like ice on white-hot coals,
No fun a flu-like cold.

*Footnote: This is a poem consisting of tercets rhyming aba,
bcb, cdc, ded, efe, ff in terza rima form.*

FAME

There once was a tiger named Ezra
Who wanted to look like a zebra.
With paint black and white
He changed overnight
And became un tigre célèbre.

GEORGIE

The people queued and gladly paid,
For Georgie was the best.
They could not understand his ways,
So anger they suppressed.

Poor Georgie kissed the girls and ran
From bed to bed to rest;
And Georgie satisfied his fans,
For Georgie was the best.

The best of Georgie was to come,
For Georgie was the best;
But Georgie felt that he was done
So gave football a rest.

He drank, he gambled, played the bore.
Poor Georgie blamed the press.
He stayed at home, then played abroad,
For Georgie was the best.

He sought a cure to gain some pride
For Georgie was the best.
He took a wife and tried to hide;
And gave the drink a rest.

Alas, he lapsed and beat his wife;
A drunkard at his best.
The surgeons tried to save his life:
George drank himself to death.

He could not cope with all the fame,
For Georgie was the best.
But in the end he made his name
Just being Georgie Best.

*Footnote: The quatrains are in Common measure,
alternating tetrameter with trimeter and rhyming abab in
Obsessive form.*

GETTING NOWHERE

                    stop.

        full   I

          a   feel

        to   I

     come   am

          I   going

     time   round

          each   in

                    circles

Footnote: This is an example of Concrete Poetry. Such a poem is often a simple typographical design making use of the words which either embody the meaning of that design or reflect upon it.

INERTIA

Many
A
False
Step
Has
Been
Made
By
Standing
Still

Footnote: Another example of Concrete Poetry. The shape resembles a leg and a foot standing still.

ODDS ON STAKES

Two ate one
Four ate three
Six ate five
Seven ate nine.
What are the odds
On staying alive?
Two, four, six, seven, eight,
Who do we appreciate?
Eight might seem odd
Depending on the stakes.
All odds being even
I'd bet on lucky seven.

Footnote: Known as a Numbers Poem because it deals
exclusively in numbers.

RICKY

My canine friend came from the vet.
We took him in without regret.
Alsatian-Collie cross was he;
A friendly dog we called 'Ricky'.

He licked my hands when we first met
And toured the garden in the wet,
Deciding that his home was set.
I swore to him he'd always be
         My canine friend.

Whenever left, he'd sit and fret
But proved a very faithful pet.
I took him walks in pastures free;
Their streams he used to jump with me.
I doubt if ever I'll forget
         My canine friend.

Footnote: The poem is an example of a Rondeau and consists of thirteen octosyllabic lines. The first half of the first line is repeated twice; once after the 8th line and again after the 13th. The rhyming scheme is aabb, aaabr, aabbar. Written for my daughter on Ricky's 3rd birthday. Ricky was her dog.

SPINSTER'S SOLILOQUY

A miss by name complete
And missed always by life.
A maiden aunt, a friend, a guest -
Not once a bride or wife.

Evenings I spend alone.
Put out the cat and pause,
Sit down, go round the flat again;
Slippers on feet like claws.

I read armchair romance
About sweet love and flowers.
A virgin's mouth with cups of tea
Sipping away the hours.

I neither smoke nor drink.
I hope I have no sin.
I take no chance at all to lose
And so can't hope to win.

Footnote: The poem consists of quatrains in Hymnal short measure, composed of two trimeter lines followed by a tetrameter and a trimeter, rhyming abcb.

THE WALL OF TIME

The wise remarks of men made famous by their words
Stand in line upon the Wall Of Time for all to read.
The world looks on, not knowing what the letters say,
For time has passed them by and people rot away.
The words upon the Wall spell out:
"WE LOVE TO LIVE AND LIVE TO LOVE."
So come, forsake all else and you will gain the world
By giving all you have to give.
Immortal phrases scribed by men of old,
Inspired by unknown people, places, things,
Remain when their contemporaries are dead and gone.
We see a part, the whole moves on,
Until the days of Revelation dawn;
When all the mysteries of life shall be revealed
And then the people by the Wall will understand.
All love once lost, the world will mourn.
The Wall Of Time, eternal in its glory, spirals
Upwards to the heavens, winding higher
With ever-increasing circles, it surrounds
The universe of distant sights and sounds;
While senses, mortal, fallible, untrue,
Inform us that the knowledge which awaits
Inside the gates of space, beyond this day and hour,
Is purified with every heart and mind made new.
The path around the Wall is littered with the mounds of bones;
The empty shells of genius once used to build the words
"WE LOVE TO LIVE AND LIVE TO LOVE."
Come, view them from above,
Then shout them out and hear the echo-call.
The Earth may shake, foundations rock,
And all may be destroyed, except
The Wall Of Time, for that will never fall.

*Footnote: An example of a Mystic Poem, which means
different things to different people.*

46

THE WAY

Since she is too blind
To find her way, I would pray:
"Lord, forgive this child
And lift her to thy bosom
So that she might see the light".

Footnote: This poem is an example of a Japanese Tanka. It consists of five lines. The first and third lines have five syllables each and the others have seven.

TO TELL THE TRUTH

Whate'er I write,
I tell the truth.
You may not like
Whate'er I write.
You look a sight!
Let this be proof,
Whate'er I write,
I tell the truth.

Footnote: This is an example of the Triolet poem; a poem of eight lines and rhyming abaaabab. The first, fourth and seventh lines are identical, so are the second and eighth.

WEEPING WILLOW

Morning, afternoon and night,
Here I'm rooted to the spot.
Casting shadows in the light;
Weeping is my chosen lot.

Here I'm rooted to the spot,
In the garden at the front.
Weeping is my chosen lot.
When gales rage I bear the brunt.

In the garden at the front,
My arms reach down to touch the ground.
When gales rage I bear the brunt;
The only time I make a sound.

My arms reach down to touch the ground,
Making real my worldly fears.
The only time I make a sound,
I'm moved to mourn the passing years.

Making real my worldly fears
With every passing friend and foe,
I'm moved to mourn the passing years;
I stand and shed soft tears of woe.

I stand and shed soft tears of woe,
In silence weep sweet tears of joy
With every passing friend and foe,
For each new baby girl and boy.

Footnote: The poem is a Pantoum; a poem of indeterminate length consisting of quatrains rhyming abab. The second and fourth line of each stanza form the first and third lines respectively of the follow stanza, except in the last stanza where they become the third and first lines respectively. There are few Pantoums in English.

WESTERN MAN

In Western Man there is an urge to rationalise
The mystic powers of Nature wherever he can;
Equally, we see the instinctive need to nationalise,
                                    In Western Man.

From the realities of the unseen world he ran,
Hiding in countries he worked to industrialise;
Shedding childlike reverence, sacred awe, for'
                                    "Scientific" plan.

Sophisticated modern aids dimmed his orthodox eyes
To the invisible mysteries of life he once scanned.
Now he is blinded by the loss, leaving much to materialise
                                    In Western Man.

Footnote: The poem is an example of a Roundel. It has nine lines divided into three stanzas. The first phrase of the first line is repeated at the end of the first and last stanzas. The rhyme scheme is aba(b), bab, aba(b). I wrote it after reading 'The World Atlas of Mysteries' by Francis Hitching.

SOME POEMS WRITTEN AS SONGS AND VICE VERSA

COLOUR BLIND IN '59

A member of our Commonwealth
A Britisher like me
Arrived in England.
He tried to find a house or flat,
Somewhere to stay
But the problem was his colour,
It was black.

We advocate equality,
We teach it in our schools.
Equality for all.
Some people slammed their doors at that,
No room for more.
The problem was his colour,
It was black.

At last he found a place to live,
The landlord called it 'home'.
A tiny room.
The walls were soaking front and back,
But never mind,
You paid a little extra
Being black.

He found a job to pay his way.
His education sound,
His word his bond.
There was nothing that this man did lack
Except one thing,
For when it came to colour
He was black.

The white man had his pride to keep,
The black man had the same
But not his freedom.
The neighbours never called him "Jack"
They called him "Coon".
The reason was his colour,
It was black.

God made the races four in all:
Pink, yellow, red and brown,
Bestowed with love.
He blessed them all, the world to pack
With mortal souls.
There are no colours
White or black,
So racists you've been told.

Footnote: Originally written as a song in 1964 which I first performed publicly accompanying myself on guitar at an evening concert held at Netteswell Comprehensive School, Harlow in Essex in July 1966.

DEEP IN THE NIGHT

Deep in the night when there isn't a sound
I lay awake and I look all around
Thinking of you and the love I have found.

I open my eyes,
I hear all your sighs.
I see a smile on your face,
I feel your warm embrace.

Deep in the night when I'm feeling down
I wonder if our love is profound.
Wherever you go, I worship the ground.

Then, time seems to fly.
Then, morning is nigh.
I'm woken by the sun.
My dreams of you are gone.

Time to get up and go;
Dreams which you'll never know,
Rising from deep in the night.
I know that we'll be together tonight.

Walking along I look at the sky.
Full is my heart, hoping you're mine.
I think of you and the love in your eyes.

Then, doubts fill my mind.
Then, I cannot find
Words to express my fears,
When you are nowhere near,
Deep in the night when there isn't a sound.

DESTINATION UNKNOWN

I came only to
Say that I cannot
Stay.
I'm so lonely it's
Time I was on my
Way.
People are strange
And they don't like to change
Unless they can have their way.

If you need me you
Only have to give the
Word.
If you want me I'll
Fly back swift as a
Bird.
Things are the same,
Like the sound of a plane,
And the words we've already heard.

I feel empty and
That I cannot
Deny.
You have plenty and
I know the reason
Why;
You take up a man
And you get what you can
While there's nothing money can't buy.

No point in stopping
When everything's rotting
As we drift slowly apart.
Like ships in the night,
We pass by the light
Of the moon, in the dark,
Destination unknown.

Footnote: Written at Axminster School. Later put to music for the School Folk Group.

EACH TIME

Each time I see the sun is shining,
Each time I see the moon is rising,
I watch to see if you are crying
And wait to find out what you're hiding.

Each time I hear your voice a'sighing,
Each time I hear the babies whining,
I wait to find out what you're doing
And wonder who it is you're fooling.

Seems I've been a fool believing.
Seems it's only me you've been deceiving.
Now I find out that you're going,
Loving someone else without my knowing.

Don't know what it was went wrong.
Thought I was the only one.
Seems I've been a fool for trying.
Seems it's only time that I've been buying,
Now I've found out you were lying,
Telling me I was the only one.

EDUCATION

Parents in the land
Tell their kids to give a hand,
Get up, get out and earn some dough,
What do you think your education's for?
We want to get on and you should too;
Get up, get out and join the queue,
Join the rat race, get what you can,
Twist and steal and dodge the man.
Rent man, tally-man, papers to pay,
All by credit, day to day.
Everybody's doing it, all the nation:
Get what you can with education.

Teachers in the schools,
Teach their pupils all the rules.
Learn this, pass that, like A.B.C
Don't you know your education's free?
Swot all the facts to learn and learn,
Then one day you'll be able to earn,
Lots of money to spend and spend;
Money can buy you many a friend.
Keep on going from day to day,
Work hard, work fast, no time to play.
All the kids throughout the nation,
Get a good job with education.

Yobs and Dropouts all,
Gather round my little stall.
Drugs and pills I have to sell,
Can't you see your education's hell?
Drives you mad with all the chore,
No social life, no life at all - it's all a bore.
Mum's at Bingo, Dad's not here -
Watching tele with a glass of beer.
No time to think, no time to pray,
God forgive us day to day:
All the people in all the nation,
Think again on Education.

Footnote: Originally written as a song which I first performed publicly accompanying myself on guitar at an evening concert at Netteswell Comprehensive School in July 1966.

IT'S A BORING ROUTINE

It's a boring routine
Getting dirty things clean.
Every day it's the same
Till my lover comes home again.

Monday morning,
Get up in plenty of time,
Get the kids off to school
In a bit of a rush.
Got to get the washing out
On the line.

Gather the clothes,
Hoping the weather stays fine.
Do the shopping in town
In a bit of a rush.
Got to get the washing out
On the line.

Washing machine
Hums and gives me the sign.
Throw in the dirty old clothes
In a bit of a rush.
Got to get the washing out
On the line.

Into the dryer
Which spins and makes a whine.
Take a trip out the back
In a bit of a rush.
Got to get the washing out
On the line.

Monday evening
My lover comes home on time.
Get the kids off to bed
In a bit of a rush.
Then bring the washing in
Off that line.

It's a boring routine;
Well you know what I mean!
Every night it's the same
When my lover comes home again.

Footnote: First written as a poem in 1973 and later put to music as a folk song.

KING ARTHUR

King Arthur was of lowly birth
He was by Merlin made.
Tintagel Castle was his home
And fighting was his trade.
He fought the Saxons and the Scots,
He sought the Holy Grail.
He held his court at Camelot
With knights so bold and brave.

King Arthur was a Cornishman
And noble were his aims.
He ruled with Guinevere his queen
And for her beauty paid.
He fought the Irish and the Danes,
He sought the Holy Grail.
Merlin made him a magic sword,
Excalibur by name.

King Arthur beat his enemies
And never made them slaves.
He taught them justice with his sword
And freedom freely gave.
He fought the Romans and the French,
He sought the Holy Grail.
His knights were faithful, but alas
Was by his wife betrayed.

King Arthur went away to fight
And left his queen to reign.
His nephew Mordred came one night
And with the queen did lay.
As soon as Arthur and his knights
Were told the sorry tale,
They journeyed home to save the throne
And Mordred he was slain.

King Arthur took a mortal wound,
His body racked with pain.
They carried him to Avalon,
His life they tried to save.
His queen sought refuge as a nun,
He sought the Holy Grail.
The Cup of Christ he came to sup
Then rested in his grave.

Footnote: Written in 1971 after I took a group of 13 year old pupils to Glastonbury, where lies King Arthur's tomb. The poem is an amalgam of all the sources (Celtic, French, British) of the legends concerning Arthur as related in 'Man, Myth and Magic' (an illustrated encyclopaedia published in weekly parts in 1970). Later put to music as a folk song.

MAN ON THE CROSS

Long, long ago, a carpenter's son
Cut all his ties with his home and was gone,
Wandering around in the heat of the sun
Carving his name on the hearts he turned on.

He questioned his elders and punctured their pride.
Their power and position he chopped down to size.
They waited to bait him, to trap him they tried,
But none could avoid the look in his eyes.

His friends were the poor and deprived of his day,
The outcasts and driftwood of death and decay.
He helped them to burn all their props and to say
"This is the life" and "This is the way".

He loosened the chains for all men to be free.
Their hang-ups he hung on that Calvary tree.
They crowned him with thorns and mocked him with glee.
"Betrayed by a kiss, king of love, come and see!"

"Oh why were you dying, man on the cross?
Why were you crying, 'lama sabachthani'?
Who could abide that man on the cross?
The blood from the nails in his flesh flowed for us.

* 'lama sabachthani' means 'why have you forsaken me?'
in Aramaic, the language Jesus spoke.

*Footnote: Originally written as a song for Axminster
School Folk Group, it was first performed at a public
concert in a hotel on Seaton's promenade in East Devon on
the evening of 19th March 1975 for Easter.*

MY DREAM OF LOVE

I love to dream my dream of love
My thoughts my own,
I walk alone
And in my walking wake the sleeping,
Dreaming of my dream of love.

And in my dream I hold no hate,
No anger to suppress.
I talk no less
And in my talking wake the dreaming,
Telling all my tales of woe.

Yet in my dream I do not suffer,
Beseeching those on high
I heave a sigh
And in my sighing wake the dying,
Breathing in my breath of life.

And in my dream I have no heartache,
No passion to control.
I rest my soul
And in my resting wake the living
Praying loud my prayer of hope.

So in my dream I sense no sorrow,
No sadness to be seen.
I live to dream
And in my living wake the loving,
Dreaming of my dream of love.

Footnote: First written as a poem in 1975 and put to music two years later.

MY GEORDIE LADDIE

I went with my Geordie laddie
For a neet oot on the toon.
We had a dance, we had a laugh
We had some Fed and Broon.
Alas the beor was too strong
And he kept falling doon.
My laddie to a netty went
Then said "Ah'll see yes soon".

I went with my Geordie laddie
To St. James's Park one day.
He said it wor a reet good treat
To watch the Magpies play.
Alas the team were all at sea
And threw the game away.
My laddie, he was sore upset
And said he couldna stay.

I went with my Geordie laddie
To the Sunday Market quay.
We stood beside the River Tyne,
He said we'd married be.
Alas, I saw it was nay good,
His heart cried to be free.
I told him so and he got mad
And said he'd go to sea.

I went with my Geordie laddie
To Jesmond Dene today.
We sat beside the waterfall,
The sky came over grey.
Alas, a Da' he was to be;
I found it hard to say.
My laddie said he had nay job
And so he couldna pay.

I went with my Geordie laddie
To his home in Benwell Grove.
He there did vow to spill his blood
But said his seed should grow.
Alas, the Tyne Bridge was the place
And there we had to go.
He planned to jump and end his life -
Then said it wasn't so!

I said to my Geordie laddie
As he walked away from me
"Weor ya gannin hinney?"
And he replied, as if surprised,
"Aam gannin heam hinney!"
I coulda cried.

*Footnote: Originally written in 1975 as a folk song and
first published in 'Collected Poems' in 2015.*

MY LOVELY MAIDEN

She was my lovely maiden
Whose eyes were bright as pearls.
She was my lovely maiden
Who loved the deep blue sea,
But now she is in heaven,
A place I'll never be.
She was my lovely maiden
And she was good for me.

My heart is heavy laden,
My eyes they smart with tears.
My heart is heavy laden
Now she has gone from me.
She didn't mind the weather
And she was lost at sea.
My heart is heavy laden,
Our love now cannot be.

We tried to find a haven,
Our hearts were filled with fear.
We tried to find a haven,
Her end it was to be;
For we sailed away together
But waves swept her from me.
We tried to find a haven,
Her haven was the sea.

*Footnote: First written as a folk song in 1976. First
published as a poem in 'Collected Poems' in 2015.*

ONE AND ONE

I'm so glad to be, I just had to be
Here in your arms.
You're so good to me and your love for me
Shows in your charms.
Way up in the sky the clouds go whistling by
As the tears in your eyes run dry.
You make me want to fly
You take me up so high.
You give me so much fun
You are my chosen one.

I don't like to be, I've no right to be
So satisfied.
You're a dream to me and I love to see
Stars in your eyes.
Way down on the ground the wind goes whistling round
While the love in our hearts abounds.
You make me jump for joy.
I'll gladly be your toy.
You're brighter than the sun.
You call and I will come.

I was slow to see, yet still hope to see
My Wonderland.
Love was dead to me then you said to me:
"Come, hold my hand."
Way over the moon, we'll dance and whistle our tune
When we tie the knot in June.
I'll give you a ring.
Together we will sing.
The bells will all be rung,
Our love songs all be sung,
As one and one make one.

*Footnote: Originally written as a folk song. First published
as a poem in 'Collected Poems' in 2015.*

PEOPLE ASK ME WHY

As I walk about the town
Feeling like a foolish clown,
People stop and ask me why
You have said goodbye.

I think of our first kiss,
You touched me to the core.
What kind of life is this,
Now we shall meet no more?

People who are they to see
How much you meant to me?
People, who are they to know
That I still love you so?

I think of our last walk.
You said that we were through.
Your love was idle talk.
Now you love someone new.

Footnote: Written as a pop song in 1960.

SACRED MUSHROOM

Sacred mushroom make me a meal.
Hector's nectar helps me grow.
Atlas Mountains reach for the sky.
Mighty mushroom, tell me why.

Mandrake magic let me feel,
Pawing flesh so silky soft.
Satan's servant bound to die,
Mighty mushroom, tell me why.

Fate-plant of the open fields,
Nature's servant of the womb,
Teaching men to live and die,
Mighty mushroom, tell me why.

Countdown to destruction, flash of fire,
Burn the flesh-plant of desire.
Sow the seeds to raise a lie.
Mighty mushroom, tell me why.

Dust to dust my destination;
Ego-tripping god of revelation,
Who is the A and O of I?
Mighty mushroom, tell me why.

Footnote: First published in '20th Century Poets' by Regency Press, London and New York in 1974. The poem is based on Professor John Allegro's theory that Christianity stemmed from an old secret Jewish fertility cult which worshipped a special coloured mushroom that sprang up overnight in their region. Originally it was published by Donovan Meher Ltd, London, as a Rock song of mine with the title of 'Mighty Mushroom'. The poem is in Obsessive form in so far as the last line in the first stanza is repeated in all the others.

SLEEPY HEAD

Rest awhile, think awhile, sleepy head.
Take your time, know you're mine, till I'm dead.
When you go, I feel low, like I said,
So rest awhile, sleepy head, in my arms.

Hold my hand, squeeze my hand, little one.
Please don't say that I may have no fun.
Play your part and your heart will be won,
So hold my hand, little one, while we talk.

Close your eyes, hush your sighs, sleepy head.
Don't you know it's time to go, time for bed?
Who can see for you and me what lies ahead?
So close your eyes, sleepy head, in my arms.

Footnote: Written in our flat in Harlow in 1964 for my wife, and later put to music as a lullaby.

TAKE MY SOUL

Sunshine and showers
Keep coming to
Colour the flowers;
Bees humming as
Church bells in steeples
Keep ringing to
Call all the people,
Birds singing to
God in His glory
Telling the story of love
Which has come from above.

Words in the Bible
Keep saying of
Life "It's a cycle";
Men praying in
Temples of Satan,
Keep leaving to
Search for their Maker;
Hands reaching to
God in His glory
Telling the story of love
Which has come from above.

Creatures of Nature
Keep dying by
Others who hate them;
Mass crying while
Armies of martyrs
Keep bleeding to
Death for their daughters,
All leading to
God in His glory

Telling the story of love
Which has come from above.

Lord be in my mind.
Teach me to be kind.
Lord be in my heart
And make a start;
Make me new, make me true,
Make me whole, take my soul

*Footnote: Originally written as a song (hymn) in 1976.
First published as a poem in 2015.*

SOME SPECIAL OCCASION POEMS

A DIALOGUE WITH MATRON

(On The Death Of My Father)

Who is that imposter in my father's bed?
He looks so ill. He seems half-dead.

It is your father and he is quite dead
He passed away just like I said.

O don't be daft. It's a waxwork dummy;
A sick joke I find not funny.

We thought it best to lay him out
In order to allay all doubt.

What happened to his bottom set of teeth?
His upper and lower lips don't meet.

We couldn't fix a smile upon his face
'Cause we found his dentures much too late.

But his mouth's half open like a fish
And he still feels warm and not quite stiff.

It can't be helped, we're short of staff.
To hunt for teeth? Don't make me laugh!

I know that Matron but my father dear
Was much too nice to wear a sneer.

If that's the case, think not it's him
But an imposter of the man within.

78

I told you so. He is not dead.
That's only his shell upon the bed.
His mask of death looks so grotesque,
At least his soul is now at rest.

ALL SAINTS, KIRKBY MALLORY

Come, let us congregate in communal joy,
To celebrate this great Festival of Flowers.
Let All Saints be filled with lavish songs of praise
And old church bells ring to herald God's hour.

Man born of woman full of noise and woe,
Be still! Hark the silent witness of the flowers!
They toil not to adorn themselves in splendour
Nor don crowns of pride to advertise their power.

Rejoice in their richness and abundance of blooms.
Like our own frail flesh, holding goodness within,
They flourish then wither, colours slowly fade,
The pleasure they give, unstained by man's sin.

Flowers carved in cedar wood embossed in gold
Adorned Solomon's Temple, symbolically sound;
Tokens of victories, remembrance and love;
Gifts we can honour on Byron trod ground.

Feast eyes and keen senses on hues by the score,
Variety in texture, fragrance and line;
Each one unique like the family of Man.
There is much to be gained if we give them our time.

Footnote: This poem was specifically written for the first celebration of a Festival of Flowers to be held at the church for the first time in 21 years. The first recitation was given in All Saints Church on the 31st August 1991. It is written in Hymnal Long Measure rhyming abcb.

AN ISLAND EXPERIENCE

There was a time when passion made my stomach
Do a somersault;
When aching limbs and throbbing heart
Made fire within my soul.
But now the ticks of time have slowed me down
And worn away the fuse to blow me up inside;
So now I know that I am growing old.
The uncertainty of youth
Which once could cause distress
Has grown to be a steady anchor in the waters
Of my decaying prime.
Like a boat long-moored, which breaks up and rots,
Its timbers floating on a wearing sea no tide can stop,
I'm helpless but at one with time.

That sure footed arrogance peculiar to youth
Which helped me climb the highest cliffs
Whose rocks were thousands of millions of times
Older than myself;
Which made me think I could compete with Nature
And succeed;
To conquer all, I understand,
Was just an ego-tripping cry for help,
Desperate to prove myself a man.

The rocks and sea will still be here when I am gone.
Now I must learn to crawl back to the sea.
No further hope of being washed up on the shore.
No wasted dreams to tie me any more,
For I am conquered by the One Who gave me birth.
This island home I must desert
On a one-way trip, never to return
I kiss the rocks goodbye.

*Footnote: I helped take a party of 34 boys and girls from
Axminster School to Drake's Island Adventure Centre in
Plymouth Sound in the Easter holiday of 1972. I wrote this
poem while sunbathing on top of the island after climbing
up a rock face to get there.*

CAPE VERDE ISLANDS

Ten volcanic islands in the corral
Offer protection from attack,
As huge Atlantic rollers sap morale
Of sailors when they are beaten back.

A jewelled ring; such a dazzling sight
Sparkles in the tropical sun.
Snow white rippled sands reflect bright light
Amid shifting dunes the prudent shun.

Constant trade winds sway verdant palms
While azure skies and turquoise seas
Display their Afro-Caribbean charms
Urging all to cast off care and wander free.

Footnote: Written on 27th January 2013, the same day I wrote 'Boa Vista', while holidaying on the island.

CARVE UP ON THE MOTORWAY

Steel sharp razor cars
Cut into the soft blotchy flesh of fog.

Ahead,
Pimples of red light
Stand out like familiar features of a face.

Taught hands tightly grip
The instruments of life and death,
Skilfully guiding them with surgeon-like precision,
Tracing the outline of the hard shoulder.

Laser beams of light converge,
Peeling the layers of skin
(Some thick, some thin)
Before incision.

Accidentally,
Knives meet sharply
Deep down inside the body.
Pools of blood slowly congeal in the still air.
For a time the flow stops
And the arterial road remains blocked
By the resulting embolism.

Footnote: _First published in 'The Inquirer', London on the_
23rd October 1976. Written after driving my car from
Weston-Super-Mare to Chard in thick fog at night on the
M5 motorway in November 1975.

CHARD 750

Information broadcast in the local press,
Invitations to the party all are sent:
"Come, celebrate this birthday of the Borough,
Join us in this joyous event."

In response we venture out
Through biting wind and flurries of snow.
Family groups with friends and neighbours
Wend their way with heads held low.

'Gainst bitter cold we cling together,
Up Snowdon Hill we climb in darkest night.
The bonfire beacon beams a welcome,
Lighting underfoot the slush and ice.

Excitement, with each heartbeat rising,
Fields now dressed in virgin white.
Crowds assemble round the toll-house;
Hundreds waiting for a light.

Time plods slowly to the nineteenth hour,
While babbling voices reach new heights.
Eager hands hold high the flaming torches;
All seven hundred and fifty now alight.

The maroon goes up, bang on the dot.
The cry goes out, "We're on our way";
Step back to the year Twelve-Thirty-Five,
To January and it's fifteenth day.

Some dressed in medieval garb
And some decked out in fancy dress,
Descend the hill in a river of light
Meandering down to the waiting guests.

Banks of people line the pavements.
Procession flows two thousand strong.
Burning rope and tallow fill the nostrils.
Chard Concert Brass, Pied Piper to the throng.

Bishop Jocelyn first gave Chard it's Charter,
And as we pass the house which bears his name,
I spy a mother with her daughter, injured,
Knock upon the door for help, in vain.

Down, down to the centre of the town we trek,
To the Guildhall with its face washed clean.
The clock tower bell tolls out its greeting,
Spectators cheer and clap and scream.

Majorettes march past with torchlight bearers,
Young and old alike now gathered there.
Upon the balcony of the Guildhall
In the spotlight, stands the mayor.

The festive scene is scanned by T.V. eyes,
Town crier cries "Oyez, Oyez, Oyez."
Pinpoints of light like birthday candles;
One for each year to the very day.

A fanfare shrills the cold night air.
The crowd is hushed, attention drawn.
The chairman of proceedings, Mervyn Ball,
Announces a year of celebrations born.

"Happy Birthday to Chard" we all sing out.
Snow falls like icing on the cake.
Torches are doused like candles blown.
"Let the fun begin with fireworks at eight."

Then after the show and the barbecue,
Like lovers wined and dined and wooed,
We tottered home without a care,
For this was Chard in party mood.
Memories of celebrations, all to share,
Now each can say that "I was there!."

Footnote: First published in 'Chard 750: A Commemorative Anthology of Selected Poems' published by the Dillington Writers Circle, Chard, in 1985.

DURHAM REVISITED

Durham, sojourn like a game of chess;
From a poor pawn's plight to a castle's keep,
From a good knight's rest to a bishop's seat.
Probe, explore and ponder every door.

Find bed and board as an opening gambit,
Allowing easy movement and access
To the quaint old city's attractions
Which its buildings and narrow streets possess.

Founded by the monks of Lindisfarne
Who fled the Viking raiders of Holy Island
And took St. Cuthbert's body to safety inland
With their sacred relics and Gospels.

They settled on a tear-shaped peninsula
High above a crook-shaped bend in the Wear.
There the massive Norman cathedral stands
Marking the spot, awesome, without fear.

It houses the tomb of the Venerable Bede.
Yet after the battle of Dunbar
Scottish soldiers were imprisoned there;
Many died, their advance well checked.

The Castle, once home to the prince bishops:
Each had his own army, coinage, courts and crest;
Noble rulers of a palatinate,
Their limitless powers had to be checked.

Descend the majestic promontory
To the wooded inner bank, quite near,
And stroll to the old mill by the weir,
Now home to ancient Durham artefacts.

On Wednesday afternoons, school and college
Coxless pairs, and fours and eights, are stretched
Out on the river to Prebend's Bridge,
Where both crews and boats are checked.

Walk the outer bank of the river's crook
From bridges Elvet to Framwelgate.
Enjoy the very finest views to date,
Amble on to shops and pubs and Market Square.

Moving on past Claypath ascend the Gilesgate hill,
Turn right and drop down to the towpath.
Student regattas and long romantic triests;
Nostalgic memories strewn along the footpath.

Boathouses, colleges of Academia,
The old racecourse and sports ground, ever green;
The famous Durham Miners Gala scenes;
Old images, new ones keep in check.

Out to the west lies the railway station;
London to Edinburgh, East Coast Main Line.
Adjacent, the soaring viaduct holds
A signal, where trains are checked sometimes.

Above the station stands Wharton Park;
A terraced area with panoramic views
Across the whole city in all its hues.
The park boasts its own castle-shaped folly.

Finally, before you leave this place,
Before checking out of your hotel,
Remember, some people find chess is ace
While others find it hell.
So whether or not you play,
Don't forget to pay
The old fashioned way
By cheque
Mate!

Footnote: Written on 30th April 2003 in Room 3 of 'The Knight's Rest'. A B&B in Durham city where we stayed a couple of nights.

HEADS AND TALES

The wide oceans,
The high mountains,
The trees in the woods,
Have stories to tell –
If only they could.

The leaves on the trees,
The fish in the sea,
The birds in the sky,
Have tales to tell –
If only they'd try.

The rocks on land,
The desert sand,
The flowers in bud,
Have stories to tell –
If only they would.

Clouds in the air,
Waves on the water,
Spray in the wind
Sweep over my head
Telling their tales
In a howling gale.

Footnote: Written after watching the film 'The French Lieutenant's Woman', and standing at the end of the Cobb on a very windy day in Lyme Regis, like Meryl Streep in the film.

HOSPITAL FOOD AND NEW BUILDING

Dear Chef of the Day
(Or Clerk of the Works)
We received with joy
Your little jest;
A brick for pud
Which was a treat
Though far too difficult to eat.
We were well on the mend
In peaceful Ward 5
Until we attacked
Your 'Concrete Surprise',
Then out came the teeth
Dented and broke
Trying to eat
Your Health Service joke.
Now we have lock-jaw,
Gums that are sore,
Unable to speak,
We can't ask for more.
When rushed to the loo
From swallowing a morsel
We left our 'deposits',
The 'bricks' and the 'mortar'!
Is this how we play
Our part in the game,
By supplying the builders
Outside with the same?
Next time you cook
Can we please have a hammer
To break up the crust
In appropriate manner?

A fork and a spoon
Are really no use.
Better a drill,
Pneumatic of course!
Then all can appreciate
Your comical works,
As we lay in our beds
Enjoying 'the perks".

Footnote: I wrote this poem at my wife's bedside while visiting her post op in Musgrove Park Hospital, Taunton, Somerset, where all the women patients were complaining about the food and the noise made all day by the builders outside.

LOVE

Love is more than kinship,
Love is more than companionship.
Love is growing togetherness,
Love is knowing madness;
Love is in the mind,
Love is blind.

Love is more than lusting,
Love is more than trusting,
Love is meeting needs.
Love is shown in deeds;
Love is in the giving,
Love is living.

Love is more than demanding,
Love is more than understanding,
Love is needing each other;
Love is being another.
Love is in the sharing,
Love is caring,

Love is.

*Footnote: The poem received its first public recitation
during our eldest daughter's marriage ceremony in St
Peter's Church in Heysham in September 1997. The poem
consists of sestets rhyming aabbcc and is an example of
Obsessive form in its repetition of 'Love is'.*

NOT CRICKET

It wasn't cricket,
Thought the bowler
As he ran up to the crease
And bowled the last ball of the over.

He had finished with her -
Though he had made promises
And she was expecting his child.

"Over" shouted the umpire.
True,
Thought the bowler
As he continued playing the game.

The crowd of spectators applauded their idol -
He'd bowled another maiden over.

Footnote: Written immediately after umpiring a school cricket match at Weston-Super-Mare Boys Grammar School.

POTS OF GOLD

There's a rainbow over Glasgow
And another over Looe.
The problem, how to link them,
Is solved by but a few.

Yet, within our little island
We find, closer to the hub,
A group of hardy whackers:
The Friendly Golfing Club.

They speak of Bogies and Birdies
And Albatross which never fly,
Sinking putts and chips that roll
And drives which reach the sky.

They tell of competitions
And of contests closely fought;
Games won and tournaments lost,
All in the name of sport.

The arching rainbows promise not
Some eternal sunny road,
But the friendships at their ends
Are shining pots of gold.

Footnote: Written specially for a golf club's annual dinner.

QUESTIONS ABOUT LIFE

If there was no creation
Why do we create?

If there was no purpose
Why do we act with purpose?

If there was no reason
Why do we have reasons?

If there was no plan
Why do we make plans?

If there was no intelligence
Why do we use intelligence?

If nothing has value
Why do we worship?

If there was no image
Why do we imagine?

If there was no right or wrong
Why do we have conscience?

If there was no God
Why do we try to act like gods?

If there was no perfection
Why do we seek to be perfect?

If there was no salvation
Why do we have faith, hope and love?

If there was no after-life
Why do we go on hoping?

If there was no beginning
Why should there be an end?

If there was ever nothing
Why is there anything?

If life was an accident
Why isn't everything accidental?

If there was no choice
Why do we have freedom?

If there were no answers
Why are there so many questions?

Footnote: Written after an RE lesson with 13 year olds at Axminster, the same day I wrote the poem 'Stars'. The poem is constructed of two-line stanzas known as "distiches" where they do not rhyme and "couplets" where they do. Used by Charles Causley at his school assemblies in Cornwall.

SWAN SONG

Super Mute Swan with crooked neck
Sitting on her nest of down
Tied by the instinct to survive,
Swaddling her cygnets five.

And on the coiling wind
Echoes of a bass guitar
Belting sounds conveyed by currents of air
Across silent fields to animal ears elsewhere.

Noise like the beat of a soldier's drum
Hammering the brain, smothering thoughts,
Blotting out both fear and foe
Projected from the darkness of the disco.

When I succumb, the urge to sing
Electrifies notes in my throat.
Pray that my chords be not too long
Nor my song too strong for the Swan.

Footnote: _Written after one of our many visits to_
Charmouth in Dorset where mute swans and their cygnets
were nesting on the river Char on an island near to the
bridge over the river at its mouth.

THE FISHERMEN OF CALDEY

We went to see the dropouts
On the Isle of Caldey.
Some of them were holy
And others had simply
Dropped in for the day.

We went by boat from Tenby
The "fishermen" to see.
While some caught dabs at sea
Others were on dry land,
Odd-men-out making scent.

We landed at the slipway
And spied a sign for shortbread.
Some people went well-fed,
Food provided daily,
While other people starved.

We entered the island shop,
Packed full of souvenirs
And gifts to ward off fears.
Chocolate sold like hot cakes;
A brand new 'Bread of Life'.

The Christians were all trading
Selling their wares for cash.
The House of God can't last
Coining money like a mint,
As in the Temple yard.

We visited the lighthouse.
The keepers all were gone.
No shining light was on.
No one to show the way.
The monks were all at prayer.

I entered the monastery
Seeking spiritual life.
I couldn't take my wife;
Women were excluded.
I felt that way within.

The monks take vows of silence,
Obedience and chastity;
A cloistered fraternity
With masochistic needs
Hidden behind closed doors.

We left the Isle of Caldey,
Our pilgrimage was done.
Refreshment, we found none.
Where were those "fishermen",
Not catching fish but men
Who served the Holy One?

Footnote: Written after a boat trip to Caldey Island while on a family holiday at Tenby. 'Caldey' means 'cold' in Viking. Dabs are the main fish caught in the area. Caldey has its own monetary unit, the Dab. The monks make perfume, shortbread and chocolate on the island.

THE ONE AND ONLY

On my journey home
I passed by way of Laugharne
And there
Along the Cliff Road
I came upon a boathouse
Where for fifteen years
Until his death in '53
Lived the "one and only"
Welsh bard.
Alas
I could not enter
The garden nor the house
For the cost
Was more than I could raise.
I consoled myself
By taking in the panoramic views
Across the estuary of the Taf
As he had done
A thousand times before.
I wandered back
Along the lane
And found the simple wooden shed -
His sanctuary -
Where he had written
Millions of words
With poor reward
Which still survive
Though he is dead.

Further on along the lane
A man
Well on in years
Was seated on a wall
Resting from his brushing up
And hedgerow cutting.
As l passed by
He smiled
And greeted me
A cheery "Good day".
I stopped in my tracks.
He touched his cloth cap.
I replied in kind
And asked if he knew
The way to the grave
Where the great man lay.
"Aye" said the old man,
"I knew him well, poor boy.
Such a nice boy he was too.
Used to walk down this lane here.
Saw him almost every day.
Moody he was too.
Sometimes he'd be full of the joys of spring
And stop and pass the time of day.
Talk for hours he would.
Other times
He'd pass by
And ne'er speak a word.
Shy, see.
Sensitive too.
Pity he had to die
To be famous.
When he was alive
Never had two pennies to rub together
He didn't.

No.....
All that business
About him being an alcoholic -
Absolute   rubbish, see.
Never had enough money for drink.....
All a myth.

Oh aye.
'Twas the drink that killed him though.
Drank a bottle and a half of whiskey
So they say.
Would have killed the strongest man.
Only thirty-six he was too.
Nobody ever heard of him
When he was alive.
Then they started coming
In the summer
After he'd gone.
Pilgrims.
Now they come
Summer and winter
From all over the world.
Had a girl of sixteen here the other day.
Come over from Canada
She did.
Said she hitch-hiked all the way.
No wonder there's so many murders about.
Ask for it
Some of 'em do."
He leaned on his walking stick
Bent like his legs
Riddled with arthritis.
His big brown eyes
Moistened a little
As they stared at me

In vacant expression.
"Aye" he muttered
As if to himself.
"Pity he had to die like that
To get famous.
Buried in the churchyard he is
Out on the St.Clears road.
If you go that way
On your right
You'll see St.Martin's church.
There's a car park there.
You'll find some steps going up.
Go up the steps
And 'cross the bridge.
There, on the other side
In the centre of the field
Is a simple wooden cross.
Painted white, it is.
Surrounded by great marble tombstones
In memory of others.
It's the only wooden cross there.
Too poor for a proper headstone, see.
That's where you'll find
The one and only."
I thanked the old man
And he shook me by the hand.
"Aye" he sighed
As I went on my way.

Footnote: We visited Laugharne on our way home from Tenby where we had been on holiday and the above is an accurate account of what happened. It was a very moving experience to walk in the shadow of Dylan Thomas and to visit "Under Milk Wood" itself. For some reason the writing of this experience distressed me greatly.

TOWARDS A JUST SOCIETY

No law can change the hearts of men
Nor put the world to rights;
Just educators know not when
Their pupils see the light.

Where unequal opportunities
And discouragements are rife,
We need a fairer share of inequalities
To supply just "tickets" for life.

*Footnote: Written for an M. Ed essay at Exeter University
on the subject of "Equality and Inequality in Education".*

TYPING

Typing is writing
Mechanical fashion
Letters in fetters
Released by the hand.
Notions in motion
Float across keyboard
Passing from mind
Into matter in bands.
Ribbon well hidden
Printing black words,
Posted to people
In far-away lands.
Carriage release
And carriage return,
Round paper bail
Shifting its stand.
Rivers of figures
Flooding the page
Ripple the surface
Channelled by man.
Typing like writing
Is tiring and testing
Hard on the hands
As scouring black pans.

Footnote: Written during an evening Typing class at Ilminster Adult Education Centre in Somerset.

UNITED

United scored and won the game.
Supporters cheered and waved their arms.
The players hugged and kissed and danced about,
But it still meant relegation.

Later, inside the changing room
When all the dirt and blood and sweat
Were washed away, the players dressed and
Each sat silently waiting.

The manager came in to give the news:
The Board of Directors had decided
That he and half the players would have to go.
United once, now divided.

*Footnote: Written at the end of the 1973-1974 soccer
season when Manchester United were relegated from the
First Division (as it was then) for the first time in 37
years. It was the end of an era; Bobby Charlton, George
Best and Denis Law had all left Old Trafford the previous
season.*

WELCOME TO GOD'S WORLD

Welcome to God's world.
Full of beauty, wonder and mystery.
Alas, there is a war on
Between Good and Evil.
Evil triumphs where Good men
Stand by and do nothing,
So fight the Good fight
With all your might
To make things right.

It started when Cain killed Abel,
but the Good have a secret weapon.
It is called Love.
It can defeat all Evil.
Practise makes perfect every day;
That is the one and only way.
Love each and every one
Until the war is finally won
And all the ugly stains of Evil gone.

Footnote: Written on the 16th October 2019 for baby Noah James Clarke's naming ceremony.

WHEN YOU ARE BORED

When you are bored
Let time stand still and think a while
Of me and of love stored
In these few words, which with a smile
You may reflect upon and know
That I am with you when you're bored.
Let time pass by and fill your mind
With thoughts of love sweet absence finds;
For love is life and life renewed.
Remember this when you are bored
With nothing else to do but brood;
For I am with you, love restored,
Till time betwixt us is no more,
And here I sit, right by your side,
For love, it knows no law.
And so as always I abide,
In thought and word, with you,
This moment..... when you're bored.

Footnote: This poem was the second one I ever wrote. I wrote it in the front room on my first visit to Marjorie's home in Newcastle. It was Easter 1960. I wrote it inside her Rutherford High School for Girls text book of Twelfth Night and she still has the copy today.

EDUCATIONAL / INFORMATION POEMS

ACTIONS SPEAK

Love and care are more oft caught
Than by some formal lesson taught.
Where principle and practise meet
The paradigm makes life more sweet.

BEYOND BELIEF

Where were you in your teens and twenties?
The Gospels do not say.
You appear upon the stage
In a very mysterious way.

When baptised by second cousin John
In the river Jordan,
You meet as total strangers,
All normal recognition gone.

You started preaching in your home town.
Why did no one know you?
You must have worshipped weekly
Like any other local Jew.

Did your family not believe you?
Did it make you think twice
When they came to take you home,
Because you claimed to be the Christ?

While walking through the rose garden
Of a busy psyche clinic
A damsel lounging on a bench,
Asked, was I a patient in it?
"No. It's a friend I've come to see".
"Hello", she said, "I'm Jesus Christ,
But the staff here don't believe me".

COLOUR

If what I saw was brown
And you saw it as blue,
If we both knew it as pink,
Would you take it to be true?

If we were all colour-blind
And colours were not real,
Would it prejudice our outlook
Or change the way we feel?

Footnote: Written for a Social Education lesson on colour prejudice.

114

COLOUR TELEVISION

Most people have a television;
Most with colour, a few without.
(Artists tell me there are no such
Colours as black and white.)
Each colour T.V. has so many lines
Which you cannot see
But together form a picture,
On a screen in the corner,
Which we commonly call 'the tele'.

It dehumanises every form of life
And develops our tolerance of horror;
Of man's inhumanity to man.
Everything is edited and re-edited
And the bits remaining
Are joined together and sent out
For us to consume as we wait
Like dustbins to be filled
Sitting at home watching 'the tele'.

Colourless conversation and discussion;
In the pub, at work and at home.
People with screened vision and imagination,
Unable to think for themselves,
Who are content to vegetate, ask:
"Did you see 'Horizon' or 'Panorama',
'Man Alive' or 'World in Action'?"
They argue all the issues
Saying "It said so on the tele".

It's true that colour adds life and realism
To the pictures on the screen and
To the lives of those who cannot get about.
But even those blessed with colour T.V.
Still see aspects of life in black and white
And swear blind that what they believe
Must be right, and what they see
Must be true, without a doubt,
Because they saw it on 'the tele'.

Footnote: Written the same evening as the poems 'Little Children' and 'Knitting'. First published in Caritas Vol 46 No 42, in Dublin, Eire in 1980.

ELIZABETH REGINA

Elizabeth, descendant of the Royal House of David,
A thread three thousand years long;
Crowned on the Stone of Jacob in the Abbey,
Anointed at her coronation by Archbishop Fisher,
The same as was King Solomon by Zadok the high priest,
Whose throne God promised, would last for ever.

Elizabeth, head of the largest ever Commonwealth of
nations
These western isles, Cassiterides, once home to Druids,
Sanctuary to the ancient migrants from Assyria;
Ten northern tribes of Israel, who lost their way
Till they were led by God's firm hand to pastures new;
Selected to answer their master's call till their lives shall
end.

Elizabeth, lifelong servant to her chosen people;
A missionary nation spreading word of the one true God.
A seat of justice and of majesty, democracy and charity,
Offering shelter to the homeless, helpless refugees.
May all who dwell in our fair and noble land be blessed
By Almighty God and His servant Israel and our Queen.

FROM IONA TO NORTHUMBRIA

Columba, the leader of the Irish mission to Caledonia,
Died in the summer of AD 597 at Iona.
In that summer there arrived in Kent
The historic Roman mission
Which came to renew the Word in Britain.
Sent by order of Pope Gregory the Great
And led by the saint to be, Augustine.

From the Humber to the Forth a pagan Anglo-Saxon
King Ethelfrith, ruled the two United kingdoms
Of Bernicia in the North and Deira in the South.
In 616 he was slain in battle
Driving the Britons into Wales as if they were cattle.
His four children were alas, left fatherless,
On the coast at Bamburgh, in the Royal castle.

The thanes consulted how to save the lives
Of Eanfrith, Oswald, Oswy and Ebba, and to decide
The destinies of these three princes and princess.
The boys were all sent to Iona.
We know not about the Princess Ebba.
In the course of time she became an abbess,
And the boys, good Christian Kings of Northumbria.

Meanwhile, Ethelfrith had been succeeded by Edwin of
Deira.
He married Ethelberg of Kent and reigned over
Northumbria.
She was a Christian, and in 627 he too accepted the faith.
Alas, at the battle of Hatfield in 633
A terrible disaster struck Christianity;
Edwin was killed by Penda of Mercia and Cadwalla of
Wales,
Who ruthlessly ravaged the land, forcing the queen to flee.

Paulinus, who in 601 had been sent from Rome
To assist Augustine, took Ethelberg to Kent, her home.
They went by sea, while for a year the heathen victors
Dispensed persecution and destruction.
Eanfrith eventually returned to claim his kingdom
But was treacherously murdered by Cadwalla.
So the work of Christ remained undone.

In 634, Oswald, who had left Northumbria a pagan child
Returned, a man of thirty, zealous Christian, full of fire.
He fought Cadwalla at Heavenfield, near Hexham and won.
Before the battle his hands perfected
A large wooden cross which he erected.
Then he called his army to kneel and pray
To the true and living God and Christ the resurrected.

Oswald justly claimed Northumbria as his right
And requested help to convert his people to Christ.
He sent word to Iona for a bishop to open the door
But the first to arrive proved unsuccessful.
The missionary opportunity still lay in a cradle.
The second, a consecrated bishop came, named Aidan.
He was simple, gentle, wise and proved more able.

Footnote: *Written in the lounge of the Bamburgh Castle
Hotel in Seahouses after visiting Lindisfarne, Easter 1975.*

GRASS ROOTS

Friesians frozen on a landscape
Black and white on green.
Mamma mammals tapping pastures
Farming full of cream.
Devon milk and money flowing
Liquid paper round,
About the lush sleep of the suburbs
Floats a fluid sound.
Rattling rows of golden bottle tops
Wake dozing herds of flesh;
In glass houses pint-sized cows
Stand partly pasteurised fresh.

Inside a home at mother's breast
A baby seeks a nipple.
On heated stove the food of love
Simmers to a ripple:
Man cooing, cow mooing.
Outside, wet grass grows brittle.

This vision of a winter's morn
Fades with watching weathered eye.
While home delivered milk is mourned
Mounds of concrete and brick sprout high.
Panoramas blotched by angled roofs
Blot verdant fields blood red.
New livestock in designer boots, not hoofs,
Trample underfoot with careless tread
Young shoots of grass once free to spread
Which now lay dead beneath grey stone beds;
Ground on which fresh human herds will soon be bred.

*Footnote: Written when our youngest daughter Josie was
a baby. I love the panoramic views of the rolling hills of
East Devon with Friesians grazing, as if frozen on the
landscape.*

IT PAYS TO ADVERTISE

It HELPS ME to sell the product.
A simple formula
To motivate the buying public.
Appeal to their need for

Health,
Efficiency,
Leisure,
Pleasure, or
Security. If that doesn't work, try

Modernity or
Economy.

Create the need
Provide the product,
Sell the idea,
Advertise.
It may not help you
But it HELPS ME
To take the money out of your pocket
And put it in mine.

Footnote: Written for a lesson in Social Education.

LIMITATIONS

Amanda
The black and white Panda
Wants to fly like the Magpie.
Up she jumps
And down she thumps,
Then rubs her bumps with a sigh.
"Oh why can't I fly
Like the birds in the sky?
Do you think I'm foolish to try?"

Footnote: Written for a Careers lesson, aimed in particular at pupils with unrealistic hopes and expectations.

MIND

Mind is clear, positive and creative;
Mind is confused and chaotic;
Mind is hidden, concealed inside.
Mind is negative and destructive;
Mind is alive and can kill.
Mind causes us to mind,
So mind we must our minds.

Footnote: Written for a lesson on Mental Health, aimed at senior pupils.

MR. JONES

Mr.Jones smokes all he can.
His skin sports a nicotine tan
Which people think he gets on the Riviera.

Mr.Jones speaks with a stammer
Since his daughter, with a hammer,
Hit him between his legs around Cape Horn.

Mr.Jones plans well ahead.
He bought his wife a double bed
Because he did not like her sleeping on the floor.

Mr.Jones sits in his corner
Playing with his doll called Norma
Which, with heated breath, he inflates from time to time.

Mr.Jones delights in malice.
He bought an old pretentious palace
With the rent money extorted from the poor.

Mr.Jones sits on his throne;
A second hand loo, all his own,
Made of gold he charges visitors to view.

Mr.Jones worships all he owns.
He lives in a million different homes
Wherever love of money is to be found.

Mr.Jones has even changed his name
Because it sounded rather plain.
Now he answers to the name Smyth-Jones.

Footnote: The poem is a satire on 'Keeping Up With The Jones's' depicting materialism as a repugnant deviation.

NEWS IN PAPERS

News is now;
Tomorrow it is history.
News is facts;
Though misleading they may be.
News is people;
Who, without the how or why.
News is action:
Wars, murders and disasters.
News is fun:
Pin-ups, babies, sport and stars.

News is photographs and words.
News is 'REAL' (with a question mark).
No one argues with a camera
When it flashes light on dark.
Different headlines, different meanings;
Captions tell us what we're seeing.
Not for the reader to decide.

The news of our times
Arrives with the mail
Express fast.
Guardians of truth
Mirror the facts
About the people.
Biased observers
Telegraph tales
As we bask in the sun
And read about our favourite star.

Footnote: Written specifically for and used as an introduction in class to a lesson on Mass Media for senior pupils in Social Education.

ON BEING HUMAN

Oh Great Designer in the sky
May I ask the question Why?
When you devised the means
By which we propagate our genes,
Were you not entirely sober?
Or suffering a hangover?
It's a comical process which starts
I must confess, in physical farce.
Alas it ends in pointless pain.
Birth is messy, uncomfortable, a strain;
Agony for Mum and harrowing for Dad.
Potentially dangerous. You must be mad!
Was there really no other way
To secure our human progeny?

Unstable and many would say unsafe,
Our home is a planet with tectonic plates;
Volcanic eruptions, earthquakes and floods
(All provided by the One who loves?)
Shifting like sand deciding our fates.
Is this what's best for the human race?
When God made the Earth, He said it was good,
Yet most would rebuild it, if only they could.
We seek out cures for our social ills
And push the limits of medical skills.
For everything there is a time and place;
Maybe like nomads we are meant to roam
And secure ourselves a safer home
Somewhere out there in boundless space.

PRIDE

In earlier times when men had clubs
And lived in caves,
Gay tribes
Found it difficult to thrive.
The Spartan army
Full of pride
Fought to the last
To keep their 'other halves' alive.
Heterosexuals too
Should celebrate with pride
The genes and chromosomes
They provide
To help the human race survive.

THE LOST TRIBES

We know the whereabouts of Benjamin and Judah
But where are the missing ten lost tribes?
And what of the promises made by God to Israel,
Are they null and void? Did they not survive?

Did the tribes migrate across the whole of Europe
Then settle in these far off Western Isles?
Did their descendants take the Word of God to others
Spreading faith and hope to enlighten lives?

Did the Anglo Saxon Celtic speaking nations
Fit the role of a chosen people?
And when called upon to suffer sacrifice and loss,
Did they boast about it from church steeples?

Was Joseph of Arimathea the first to plant the seed
In this outpost of the Roman Empire,
By bringing Jesus at the age of twelve to live here,
As holy writ and legend so conspire?

Is God working out His purpose each successive year?
As a nation do we have a choice?
If so, our history and our future path are clear -
As spoken by the prophets with one voice.

Footnote: Based on the working hypothesis that the
English speaking people are the descendants of the
Ten Lost Tribes of Israel.

THE STORY OF THE DINOSAURS

Before the orogenesis
Of the Alps and Andes;
Before the Himalayas,
Rockies and Pyrenees
Folded into the blue sky;
Before Man had his birth
And wrote his name in the sand,
Dinosaurs ruled the Earth.

The Book of Earth History
Four thousand six hundred
Pages, a million years long,
Leaves a lot to be read.
The dinosaurs fill some
One hundred and thirty
While mere Man appears
On the last page only.

Humans never saw their success
Nor witnessed the decline
Of these lords of creation.
In their Triassic prime
They straddled the shrinking globe
In majestic splendour,
Dominating continents,
Paragons of power.

Elite of the Reptile Age,
With egg-brains at their core,
Two-footed and four-footed
Carnivores and herbivores;
Horned, spiked, long-necked, duck-billed,
Large, medium and small.
Some monsters walked upright.
Some crawled on all fours.

The Mesozoic era
Of prehistoric beasts,
Gave pride of place to tyrants
In tropical world heat.
Terrible lizards roaming
Upland, swamp and jungle;
Swimmers, diggers, tree-climbers,
Tearing Earth asunder.

A two-legged meat eater,
Awful Allosaurus,
Swept Jurassic landscapes
Hunting Brontosaurus.
Theropod of theropods,
Tyrannosaurus Rex,
King killer of Cretaceous,
A cannibal, came next.

Sounds of brawn reverberant
Rumbled beneath the ground,
Like distant thunder coming
When these giants roamed around;
Cold-blooded automatons
Who killed without a care.
The modern bear and lion
Are harmless dwarfs, compared.

T.Rex, with mouth a metre wide,
Armed with scimitar-teeth
And hands hooked with tearing claws,
Was truly a masterpiece:
The ultimate in brute strength,
A tale of brawn triumphant
Over brain for generations,
Till victor lay defunct.

(Dinosaurs, oh dinosaurs,
Oh why are you extinct?
Was it racial senescence
Or did you never think?
Chromosomes in chaos
Producing toothless freaks?
Who preyed upon your eggs
And relatives did eat?
Did the climate grow too cold?
Were there epidemics?
Did your food supply all fold?
Were changes far too quick?)

Evolution has its failures.
The dinosaur was one.
Compared to the dinosaurs
Man is but Tom Thumb.
Should we ever be their peers
We need to survive
Another one hundred
And twenty-nine million years.

Footnote: Written after watching a TV programme about
dinosaurs and the latest theories of how and why they
became extinct.

UNEXPECTED

Watch and pray
Night and day.
Who can say
When he will come?

He said he would come back again
To judge the living and the dead,
With power and great glory
As King of Kings and Lord of Lords to reign.

Every eye shall see him.
Suddenly, everything will change.
In the twinkling of an eye,
Some will live and some will die.

Like a thief in the night
He will come at an unexpected hour.
Was he wrong or was he right?
Only time will tell if he has God's power.

So watch and pray
Night and day,
Lest he catch you sleeping
In your disbelieving.

Footnote: Based on quotations from the Bible like John 14 v1-3 it is clear that Christ himself believed he would literally come again.

WHO IS LIKE THE LORD?

Muslims, Christians, Jews,
Monotheists everywhere,
Call me Yahweh, Allah, God
Yet drive me to despair.
We are all the same.
No need to choose -
But if I were your Creator
I would tell you now, not later,
That fighting over who is right or wrong
Is wrong and wrong, so wrong.
What kind of deity am I
Who let's you live with blinkered eye?
I did not create so you could kill.
You have misunderstood my will.
You are meant to love instead of hate.
Therein lies *your* ultimate Fate.
Wise up and put your arms away
And fill the world with peace today.
If you REALLY want to worship me
Then learn to live in harmony.

Footnote: 'Michael' in Hebrew means 'who is like the Lord?' The rest is self-explanatory.

SOME PUPILS / STUDENTS FAVOURITES

(Selected by pupils from Stockport School, Axminster School and King Edwards Grammar School, Birmingham)

A DAUGHTER'S FRIGHT

Warm and cosy curled up in bed
She woke with a start and turned her head.
The bedroom door creaked slowly ajar,
A ghostly shadow crawled up the wall.
Cold fear shivered all down her spine
As she suppressed a plaintive whine.
Had a bogeyman come to call
Or a burglar to steal her toys?
She froze and stared wide eyed in fright
When suddenly all was bathed in light.
It wasn't a phantom or a spectre out to spook,
Only Daddy looking for his Puzzle book.

A LESSON

"Line up properly.
Right
Girls first,
In you go.
Right boys
Follow on.
Stand up straight everyone,
That includes you Smith.
Sit down
Quietly!
Take out your books.
Anyone not got a pen?
You'll need your rulers.
I want you to write what's on the board,
Copy it down
Neatly into your books.
Leave a margin.
Don't forget to underline
The heading and the date.
Today, as you can see
We are going to do
'FREEDOM'.
Keep your work tidy.
Remember what I said.
What's the matter Smith?
No pen?
For God's sake lad
Why do you always have to be different?
Here, use this one……
Now what's the matter Smith?
No ruler?
God give me strength!

Who hasn't finished yet?
Right. Good.
All, except you Smith.
Hurry up boy,
We can't wait all day for you.

Everyone finished.
At last!
Now, who can define freedom for me?.....
Doing what you want?
Well, yes, up to a point.
Can anybody add anything to that?
Yes Smith?
What do you mean,
There is no such thing?

Let me explain -
Yes, I know that's the bell.
The bell is for me not you.
Now where were we....?
Oh well,
There isn't time to explain now.
Put your things away.
We'll carry on from here
Next week."

A SIMPLE MAN

I am a simple man at heart
Who enjoys the occasional fart;
For farts are fun and simply made,
Pure air their pungent smells pervade.
Some are silent, others loud,
Some disperse a gathered crowd.
Unique in pitch as well as pong
I like them more than any song.
When in the bath we liberate
And bubbles blown reverberate.
When bursting forth in packed out room
They break the boredom or the gloom,
Causing folk to glance and titter,
Keen to see who has the jitters.
Light a match and you will find
A blue flash leads to burnt behind.
Guilty party flushed with shame
Departs head down to fart again.
To those uncultured in the Arts,
The most expressive is to fart.
To a simple man it's all to plain,
No two farts are e'er the same.

Footnote: Voted the most popular poem of the pupils of Stockport School in December 2014.

BEAUTY AND THE BEAST

"You're a beauty" said he.
"And so are you" the Beauty said.
"No I'm not, I'm ugly" said he.
"Then so am I" the Beauty said.

"I love beauty" he said.
"And I love you" said the Beauty.
"Oh, it's not you I love, but your beauty" he said.
"Oh, you beast!" said she.

EARTH, WATER, FIRE AND AIR

Earth is soft and fertile;
A bed in which grow seeds
Of grain, flowers, weeds and trees.

Water is wet and flows;
The source of life and power,
It creates and destroys at will by the hour.

Fire is hot and burns;
It transfigures and transforms,
Ashes to ashes and dust to dust.

Air is invisible all around;
It is free for us to breathe,
Both still or moving at gale force speed.

The earth needs water
And the fire needs air.
Nature needs them all, so I should care
While I am still here, they are still there.

FLOWERS OF YOUTH

Flowers of youth in our good land
Rise up and catch the morning sun.
Gently fold it in your hands,
Keep it with you and have fun.
Take it before the evening comes.

Flowers growing in the sunshine
Stand up and kiss the air we breathe.
Sparkle with your budding minds,
Softly open up your leaves.
Caress the sad and lonely breeze.

Gentle flowers of youth begun,
Colour our world as we pass by.
Meadows made for you to run,
While waving to the distant sky
Taking the clouds of tears to dry.

Flowers of youth be strong and brave,
Face up and slay the common foe.
Knowing love will always save,
Take it with you when you go,
Before the winds of winter blow.

Footnote: The most usual rhyming scheme for the quintain is ababa or abaca. This poem is ababb.

GLASS EYE

I stood by a pool, dazzling,
Like a window of glass
Reflecting the sun.
I looked in the mirror
Beyond the surface
At the cool depths below,
Where I saw darting fish
And plant-like forms
Swaying to and fro.
Each in its own way
Searching for food.
But for all I could see
The water was void.
A drop from that pool
Of clear water I took
And placed on a slide.
Then I had a close look
Through a more powerful
Mechanical glass eye.
And there, invisible before,
Were many strange creatures
Swimming about.
Without a doubt
There are more,
Micro- and macroscopic,
Which remain to be seen
Through the windows of life
By the 'blind' human eye.

GO ON, TRY IT

When I was out with my love
He said "Come lie with me".
I looked at the sky above
And he asked me if I would,
Saying, "Go on, try it, go on".

A friend whom I liked a lot
Said "Share a joint with me".
She told me the stuff was hot
Before handing me some pot,
Saying, "Go on, try it, go on".

A man in The Rising Sun,
Said "Have a drink with me".
I told him I was too young
But he bought me coke and rum
Saying, "Go on, try it, go on".

Some people I know so well
Think I should be like them.
They cheat and they lie like hell.
My soul they'd love to sell
Saying, "Go on, try it, go on".

Oh no, no, no, to each and every one.
I said I wouldn't do it,
I couldn't tell my Mum.
I want to go to heaven
So I try to do no wrong.

I'M A VANDAL

I'm a vandal,
I'm a wrecker,
I'm a breaker-in-two.
I'm a yobbo,
I'm a smasher,
I'm a nuisance to you.
I'm a wilful destroyer of beautiful things.

When I'm bored and frustrated
With nothing to do
I'll wander the streets
And get kicks with my feet
By mugging a woman or two.

When I'm tired and resentful
Of people like you,
I'll go with my mates
And get rid of my hate
By smashing a window or two.

When I'm scared and confused
By something that's true,
I'll carve out my name
And prove that I'm sane
By wrecking a car or two.

When I'm high and elated
By drinking a few,
I'll paint the town red
On blank walls like my head
By smearing a letter or two.

When I'm angry and violent
I'll damage what's new.
I'll skin a few cats
Or light fires with a match
And torch a building or two.

Whatever you state,
I'm proud to relate
I'M A VANDAL, mate!

IN LOVE WITH MY CAR

(With apologies to Roger Taylor of Queen)

The machine is a dream
So clean,
With pistons pumping,
Hubcaps gleaming.
Holding the wheel
I steer with my hand
On the gear,
Throbbing with life
Racing along
In top.
Pulsating machine
Is well greased.
I've got a feel for my car
Like an obsession
And an addiction
Rolled into one.
It's a thrill
Driving my automobile.
Told my girl "goodbye"
For my four-wheeled friend
Never talks back
When I'm cruising in style,
Out to impress.

And later -
Cloth in hand,
I'm wiping it clean,
Gently polishing,
Caressing the sheen,
To mirror my face
In some masturbatory
Fantasy.
With my phallic symbol
I stand outside my door -
Steppenwolf would say
It was "For Ladies Only" -
Paying narcissistic homage.

LITTLE CHILDREN

Children live in a fantasy world
Of red-eyed monsters
Which come and eat them up
In the night;
Of good fairies
Who collect extracted teeth
And leave some money behind.

Children play at Shops, Doctors and Nurses,
And Mummies and Daddies;
Imitating and reliving experiences
They have known
Or have seen.
They live in a world of adventure
Copying all that they find.

Children live in fear of the dark
Without knowing why;
Of shapes and shadows cast
Upon the wall;
Of strange noises,
Exaggerated by the silence,
Heard in the middle of the night.

Children live in a world of make-believe,
Where everything wrong
Can be made to be right;
Where wishes
All come true.
They pretend to be people they are not
And dress up to suit the occasion.

Children accept what they are taught
Without question;
And are so conditioned by
Mummy and Daddy
And Teacher at school
(Who are fountains of truth to them)
To believe that adults are always right.

Children think that real people are not bad
And that all life is good.
Only witches, ghosts and dragons
Can do evil.
Yet they can be
Cruel to each other without caring,
And ignorant of how and why.

Children love their pets of all kinds,
From horses to dogs.
They love colours and sounds.
They believe in Jesus,
God and Father Christmas
Like little angels, who when it suits,
Can become little devils.

Children take the world for granted
As if it all belongs to them.
As they grow older the dreams
Begin to fade.
They see it as it really is
And are disillusioned by its imperfections,
Wishing all their childhood dreams had been real.

Footnote: Written on the same evening as 'Knitting' and 'Colour TV' while babysitting our two children aged two years and six years old.

LIVING LANGUAGE

Language is a life-long sentence for Man,
Made up of letters, words, paragraphs
And chapters of communication,
In the ever-open pages of the
Book of Life;
Punctuated only by illness
And death.

LOVE – HATE RELATIONSHIPS

Love

    Respect

        Parents

           Pride

               Fall

Down

    Out

        Count

           Chickens

               Hatch

Eggs

    Fresh

        Break

           Pastures

               New

Desire

    Familiar

        Contempt

           Envy

               Green

Peas

    Split

        Sides

           Opposite

               Love

Hate

Footnote: A 'Visual' poem based on word association.

MICKEY THE MONKEY

Mickey the Monkey
Lives in a tree.
He knows his numbers
One, two, three.

One for the monkey
Two for the tree.
Three for the letters
A.B.C.

Mickey the Monkey
Looks down on me.
He walked with angels
Out of the sea.

A is for ape-man
B is for me.
C is for cloning
One, two, three.

Mickey the Monkey
Can talk to me.
He told me the secret
Of Sirius B.

Was it a spaceman
Up in the tree?
Whence came the monkey
Came you and me?

Footnote: The poem is based on the idea that Earth was visited by an intelligent being from a planet in the system of the star Sirius, expressed in the book "The Sirius Mystery" by Robert K. G. Temple in 1981.

PARENTS "DELIGHT"

There was a young Cannibal called Gus
Who used to eat lettuce and stuff.
His parents said, "Son,
It's bad for your tum!
Why don't you eat humans like us?"

Gus thought for a time and made up his mind,
One had to be cruel to be kind.
"I'll do as you say
And eat meat from today"
Then he slew them both from behind.

Footnote: A poem set in Limerick form with both quintains rhyming aabba.

PERSPECTIVE

How far is a metre
To a snail?
How high is a hill
To an ant?
How great is a man
Compared to the Earth?
How small is our planet
Against the sun?
What size the sun
Compared to our galaxy,
In which there are at least
A hundred thousand million others?
What size our galaxy
In the vast universe
Containing millions of other Milky Ways?
All parts must go
In proportion to the Whole,
And we, a part,
Must find our own
Perspective.

SCHOOL CAT

She walks like a cat, aloof and sleek,
Seemingly soft, cuddly and vulnerable.
Her sharp eyes alert, catching every move;
Timid but wearing a face of stone.
This girl, in regulation blue, pads to school;
Shabby tiger, alley cat,
Carrying books beneath her arm, she purrs,
Warmed by thoughts of sensuous knowledge.
She comes for cupboard love, not to learn;
Attention like milk she laps up with hungry tongue;
She comes to take and not to give,
This earthy creature on the prowl for Tom.
At her desk she sits like Vesta in the hearth,
Body outstretched in lazy recline,
Waiting, watching over her domain,
Ready to pounce or snarl with arrogance
At some unsuspecting innocent who may disturb her peace.
This pampered pet with hidden claws of iron
Could tear out your heart
And watch the tears fall down your face,
Unmoved.

Footnote: The poem is based on a pupil in my tutor group
at Axminster. The same pupil returned to the school many
years later as a cleaner of my new tutor room before I left
teaching to do a Master's degree at Exeter University.

SOCCER GIRL

She's a true football fanatic
Everywhere you'll find her at it;
She'll give you a kick if you get in her way,
And boot the poor coach if he won't let her play
Football.

She'll play anywhere to get it,
People say she's 'energetic'.
If you want her to score just give her the ball,
Then hug her and kiss her and tell her it's called
"Football".

She's the queen of the soccer scene,
Superstar of her local team.
If you shoot her a line, she'll say she is game,
She'll always play ball if you mention the name
"Football".

Everyone thinks that she looks weird;
She's six foot six and sports a beard.
They all get a fright when she comes out to play
And run for their lives when they think it is 'gay'
Football.

She's got FIFA in a whirl,
People call her "Georgie Girl".
She's the best in all the world.
She's appeared on tele with mud on her chest;
She's a female Pele, a Matthews and Best
Of all -
'She's no boob with a ball!

*Footnote: Written for (not about) my eldest daughter
Sam who played for Chard Ladies FC at the age of
twelve in 1980.*

157

TAKE THE SUN

Take the morning sun
And fold it in your hand.
Take it with you when you go,
I'll keep the home fires burning.
You will see the seeds you sow
Growing in the land of learning.
Flower of youth so young
Shine forth out of the desert sand.
Unfold your petals and glow,
Satisfy your curious yearning.
When the heat has gone
And you're strong enough to stand,
You will fill the life-blood flow
With your experience and discerning.
Leaves will fall in autumn
As Nature does demand,
So take the sun and blow,
Before the winter comes in mourning.

Footnote: Written on the request of a school leaver, the day they left.

THE VALLEY OF THE LIVING DEAD

As I walk through the valley of the living dead,
I see the blind who cannot see the light.
I watch the deaf who cannot hear the word.
I meet the dumb who cannot talk.
Having eyes to see and ears to hear and tongues to speak
They have not learned to use their senses,
So they dwell in the valley of the living dead.
Pathetic cases of their own creation
Gathering round their shallow souls
Material possessions to fill their lives.
All hopes are based on false elation
Manufactured to create sensation,
Only to find they are bent and broken
As they walk through the valley of the living dead.
The poet who has lost his rhyme,
The minstrel who has lost his song,
The preacher who has lost his faith,
All hope that someone else will lend a hand
When finding signs they do not understand.
The scientist who lacks imagination,
The proud who strive to keep their reputation,
All are walking through the valley of the living dead.
They know not why they live.
They work to buy their happiness,
All slaves to ownership.
They flaunt their artificial beauty
Which by money they possess,
Hoping all who view their gains will feel deprived
And like them, will want for more.
Yet all the time they are slowly dying
As they walk through the valley of the living dead.
People come and people go while time ticks on.
Some have a daughter, some a son.

From all the truths of life they run.
Ignorance multiplies their guilt;
Their minds they cannot mend,
Their love they cannot share,
Their hearts are empty, bare.
Colourless characters, eyes completely blank,
With naked personalities stand
Lined up in order hand in hand
Along the valley of the living dead.

Cut short my visit to this place
Where millions gather to perform
Their roles in life unto its end.
They live, yet all the time pretend
To be what they are not.
This confused and ugly lot
Are driving me insane.
Spare me the pain
To watch them rot
In the valley of the living dead.
Dear God, on whom I call,
I do not know you much at all.
I thought I did but then the darkness came
And clouded up my cluttered brain.
Why did you lead me to this place?
Was it to understand your grace?
Release me now and let me live.
The light is bright and crystal clear.
The mist inside my head is lifting.
My eyes are moist with joy,
My freedom now I will enjoy
And new found knowledge I'll employ
In helping those who do not use their senses
To appreciate the wonder of the world
Outside the valley of the living dead.

WHERE WERE YOU?

Where were you when I sought you
Down the darkened lanes at night
And chased your shadow
Up blind alleys?
Were you ever there?
And when I wandered the streets
In hope of meeting you,
Did I really ever see you?
How will I ever know
If what I saw was true?
And when I thought I caught
A fleeting glimpse of you
Among the crowds,
I danced and dodged and bobbed
My way to where you stood.
You were not there;
I found another standing in your place.
Where did you go?
Did you know,
And run to hide your face?
Did you laugh when you saw my tears?
And when I strolled by your house,
Did I see you sitting at your window
Waiting for a sight of me?
Or were you simply there by chance?
And when I cast my eye
In your direction,
Did you want to see me
On the outside looking in?
If I'd stopped and knocked upon your door
Would you have welcomed me within?

WITHOUT RHYME OR REASON

Where is the poet for the common man
Who will use common words
To describe the common lot
Of common men?

Where is the poet for the ordinary man
Who uses ordinary words
To express ordinary feelings,
And ordinary thoughts
With ordinary meanings?

Why do poets arrest the passer-by
(Searching for a common heritage),
With minutiae extraordinary,
Babbling from their ivory towers
In Babel?

Gone the style to deal with abstract ideas
Head-on.
Gone the love of poetry
Which died
Unwon.

Found, the extraordinary man
For the common poet;
Found, the muses for the elite
And self-elected audiences.

Now you tell me:
Where is the uncommon poet
For the common man?

*Footnote: The poem was written in response to a letter to
the author from Ken Crossley-Holland, Poetry Editor and
Director of Vector Gollancz Publishing Co. Ltd London in
1975.*

POTPOURRI POEMS

A BAD START

Waning
Moonshine
On the newborn babe.
Wednesday's child,
Full of woe,
Born on an ebb tide
At sunset,
Will not have far to go.

AUTUMNAL MORNING

November dawn with sun and sky
Form shades of grey with reddish hue.
Yet slowly through a parting mist
Appears a silent orange disc,
While night time frost dissolves in dew.

Trees stripped naked, exposed anew,
Stand rigid in the biting cold.
Brittle branches like outstretched arms
Appeal for warmth, though touched with gold,
Icy drips drop like tears of woe
Down to the rotting leaves below.

Shrubs adorned in gossamer, glisten.
The garden shed hides spiders webs
Woven in corners luring prey.
Among the shrubs the birds compete
To find what treats there are to eat.

Our planet, always in a spin
Revolves like an old Roulette wheel
Deciding who will lose or win.
Random chances in life are real
As seasons deal them on a whim
And weather colours how we feel.

COMING TO TERMS

My parents confessed I was an accident
Conceived amid bombs at the height of war.
They already had three. Didn't want any more.

They said they would have preferred a girl.
They liked the names Rosalind and Rose,
To suit a wished-for scholar or lover of prose.

In fact my talents lay in the field of sport.
No family members ever came to watch me play;
"A grammar education going to waste" they'd say.

When I 'got religion' I applied to be ordained.
I quite fancied being a padre or a preacher.
The Church denied me, so I ended up a teacher.

My wife would wish me to be a practical man;
A maker and mender, helper and cleaner,
Not someone who spends his day a dreamer.

I have two lovely irreplaceable daughters
But always yearned for a companionable son.
I was told that three is unlucky for some.

Let nothing mean too much when testing Fate.
It's said that those who want will never get;
Like when we pray for sun it turns out wet.

Desire and denial, with familiar ring,
Resonate throughout our capricious lives.
Not a thing about which to rejoice or sing,
More a warning bell of what the future brings.

COVID 19

It was once said, let China sleep,
When she awakes, the world will weep,
And so it is with millions weak
And millions more who cannot speak.

No offers of help to brothers;
China shows no regret to others.
A deafening silence covers
Even the most ardent lovers.

Fight to breathe as long as you can
In this pandemic caused by Man,
Spread like fire by a walking fan
By those who do not give a damn.

Sweet kiss of death, oh so sublime,
Release me from this pain of mine.
May peace and grace of love divine
Bless all who tread the steps of time.

DESERTED ISLE

Milky sand slurped by lethargic waves
On a silk-soft carpet beach of foam.
Footsteps fast fading from the water's edge
Landward-bound, seeking a home.
Both of us abandoned on a deserted isle,
Shaded only by the sword-blade leaves of palms.
Eye-pools reflect the twinkling sun on sea.
Castaways, love-loose in each other's arms;
Open mouths word seashell sentiments,
Broken only by the taunting breeze.
Bloated lips suck in the salty air.
Entwined we stand on shifting sand.
Overhead, anvil shaped thunder clouds rise in haste,
Poised to lash an ocean wasteland.

DOUBTING THOMAS

Father Tom spent all his life preaching the good news:
Have faith or death, we have to choose.
The Gospel speaks of Paradise,
Much better than a cruise.

Tom was a travel agent sent unto the pews,
Issuing tickets to the few,
Guaranteeing ultimate bliss
And free insurance too.

One day old Father Tom consulted his GP.
The doc confirmed he had big C.
Did Thomas die in faith or fear
In so few weeks as three?

Footnote: Written in quatrains rhyming aaba
(unusual).

HEAVY SHOWER

Footsteps splattered like wet fish
On the stone pavements of the streets.
People hunched and huddled,
Darted for refuge from the sheeting rain.

I nestled in a doorway
Mesmerised by the rhythmic beat:
Pit-a-pat, pit-pat - plop.
Drips dropped from the gutters overhead.

My skin bristled up in waves
As I lolled snug in a doorway.
The water gurgled down drains
And gushed spluttering from the pipes.

The neon amber street lights
Cast a warm glow on the buildings.
Walls and roof-tops gleamed brightly.
A new-look, fresh sheen, bestowed on everything.

As the downfall subsided,
And flood-water ran off in streams
Fast disappearing underground,
I felt a slow wet trickle down my neck.

Footnote: Written on the same day as 'The Potter' and 'Lost Love'.

NORMAL SERVICE

Out of the darkness came the light.
With one look my thoughts were aroused.
In one act my anger was doused.
With one smile my world was made bright.
In one word my wrongs were made right.
With one kiss my life was restored.
In one breath I came back to life.

ODE TO THE UNIVERSE

Oh Universe, oh Universe
Your birth a mystery,
Will we ever learn your secrets
Or touch your majesty?

Oh Author of creation
Is there purpose in your mind?
Is the chaos accidental
Or the order by design?

Oh creatures of creation
Have you a mind to care?
Does it matter what is matter,
So long as it is there?

Oh Universe I learn of you
Through pupils in my eyes.
At night your flashing lights I view
Through windows in the sky.

A speck upon a speck of dust;
Islands in seas of space.
I doubt if ever nothing was
Or else this world be waste.

PUSS PUSS

She lay on the thick woollen pile
Of the carpet in front of the fire,
With her legs outstretched
And eyes half closed,
Waiting to be petted.
I knelt down beside the feline creature
So that I could touch her.
And with my palm I stroked
And caressed her silky hair,
Thinking "Oh, what a lovely pussy.
What a lovely pussy you are!"
She purred with contentment
Licking my hands,
Expressing her joy.
Later, she rose to leave the room,
Her lips half-open in a wicked smile.
And when she reached the door
She turned her head
And cast a knowing eye
In my direction.
Then, did I hear her sigh
And softly say
"Goodbye"?

TO DROPOUTS YOUNG AND NOT SO YOUNG

Where do they hide from the
Hustle and bustle,
The pace, the race?
Do they dig pits
Lose their wits,
Escape by T.V.,
Or creep away in self-contained shells
To anonymous seas?
Do they take a trip
On the mainline,
To the sunshine
Glitter-litter-land of sham?
Puzzled people, bored people,
Apathetic stereotypes,
Waiting for something to happen.
Where's the spirit which won world wars?
Where's the drive, the zeal, the gall?
Is the wheel of change turning too fast?
Are they thrown by centrifugal force
Into some inert reality?
It is a tiresome wheel
Which turns and turns
Without oil or brawn,
In no particular direction.
Blessed are those
Who do something positive,
Before they are too old
To do anything at all
And drop out for good.

WORMS

Devil's
Flesh, ripple-ringed,
Sent to work underground
Tunnels in tombs of dead silence
For good.

To search
Buried bodies
And eat away decay,
Swelling jelly-soft bellies for
Blackbirds.

Footnote: The poem consists of two stanzas in cinquain form of 2-4-6-8-2 syllables.

ZODIAC RHYMES

Aries the Ram
He stole some jam
And gave himself a treat.
The ram he fled
From farmer Fred
Who cut him up for meat.

Taurus the Bull
Thought life was dull
So bought a china shop.
The bull went wild,
In came a child
And smashed the blooming lot.

Gemini Twins
Made such a din
And quarrelled every night.
The twins they fought
Till they were caught
Then argued who was right.

Cancer the Crab
A man did grab
Out swimming in the sea.
The crab squeezed tight,
The man took flight,
"You're tickling me!" cried he.

Leo the Lion
He bought some iron
And built himself a cage.
The lion did roar,
He'd lost the door,
"I can't get in!" he raged.

Virgo Virgin
Gets in a spin
When faced with something new.
The virgin cries
She always tries
But finds "new" hard to do.

Libra the Scales
Shouts "heads" or "tails"
According to the rules.
The scales go down
Holding the crowns
Of honest men and fools.

Scorpio the
Scorpion the
Sexy, sinister thing.
He bends his back
To hide the fact
His kiss is like a sting.

Sagittarius
Gregarious,
An archer and a beau.
He twirls his curls
To slay the girls
With arrows from his bow.

Capricorn Goat
Stands by and gloats
When others take a fall.
The goat is rough,
He thinks he's tough
But listen to his call!

Aquarius,
Precarious
Water-carrying man,
Plods to and fro
Then stubs his toe
And falls into his can.

Pisces the Fish
Pose on a dish
And drink to pass the time.
The fish can't wait
And eat the bait
Until they catch a line.

Footnote: The poem is constructed of sestets rhyming aabccb of 4-4-6-4-4-6 syllabic form.

LAST ORDERS

Grieve not for me when I am gone
But fill your heart and mind with song.
Mope not nor hang your head for long
But gird your loins and journey on.

Our bodies were not made to last.
I'm stuck with mine until it's ash!
For me the future is now past.
What of my soul? I dare not ask.

Remember me, a part of you;
Hand in hand we stretched and grew,
Bonded by values shared by few,
Weaned on love in a family pew.

Be thankful for each gifted year.
Rejoice and hold each moment dear.
Treat death itself as nought to fear
And wipe away all mournful tears.

We march through history marking time
And one by one drop out of line.
Your turn will come just as has mine
So celebrate your life in kind,
Enjoy my wake, fine food and wine.

Footnote: Written after reading the novel of the same title by Graham Swift.

IN MEMORIUM POEMS (RIP)

In memory of those who encouraged, helped and supported my poetic efforts and who have now passed on.

FOR

Ruth Morris - Drink To Me Only

Jagdish Bhatt - Face The Nation

Jean Breeze - Friends

Maris Hind - In Nature's Garden

Robert Horton - Reminders

Paul King - School

George Smith, M.A - The Artist And The Mirror

Dr. A.J. Dulzell-Ward - The Knock Upon Your Door

Katharine Pinder - To The National Health 2040

Dr. Charles Causley - Tree Speech

Howard Sergeant MBE - When You Are Gone

DRINK TO ME ONLY

I was a magnum
And you kept me to yourself.
Now you are a drunkard
And you've had your fill of me.

Footnote: Written in the Red Lion pub in Axminster during a Folk Club evening.

FACE THE NATION

The face of England
Blotched and blighted,
Struck by the Architects' plague.
That face which once was
So beautifully made
Is pock-marked by cities
And inflamed conurbations.
Villages and towns like festering sores
Expand with the economic need for more.
The stain of industry everywhere,
Spreading poisons, disease and grief,
Like eating away the leper's cheek;
Eyes smarting, nose running,
Ears aching, mouth gaping,
Skin cracking, oozing pus,
Smeared with the ointment 'Pollution';
A product marketed by Evolution
To hide the parasites feeding off the nation.

Oh, Merry England, weep no more!
Have a face-lift, find a cure.
Smile again with conservation
Or pay the price, decapitation.

FRIENDS

Friends are people who will give their lives for you,
The rest are but acquaintances.
Friends are more precious than gold or silver
And just as hard to find.
Friends are more beautiful than diamonds or pearls;
Their love never fades in the darkest moments.
Friends are like rare and delicate plants
Which when found, need tender care.
Friends are more reliable than modern computers;
They give you the truth without your asking.
Friends are free and cannot be bought;
They give and do not look for any reward.
Friends will share their lives with you forever,
If you can lose yourself in theirs.
To lose a friend is to lose a little of yourself
And the world is poorer by the loss.
To find a friend helps you find yourself,
For friends make life worth living.

IN NATURE'S GARDEN

Flowers blossom in the summer sun
Then fade away in the evening shade.
Shadows of their former selves they droop,
The beauty of their youth betrayed.

In time each bloom will don its splendour
Bestowing colour on our mundane lives.
Scents and hues bombard our senses
Bringing joy to hearts and tears to eyes.

Every flower has its purpose.
Ask the bees that come to call.
When petals fold and day is over,
Remember loved ones when they fall.

REMINDERS

Christmas
Suffering Slave
Promised God incarnate
Born a babe into Bethlehem
Star-struck.

Easter
Resurrection
Branch of Jesse pruned so
New buds can grow and blossom on
Life's Tree.

Whitsun
Quickening wind
Fanning flames of passion
Transforming embers into white
Hot coals.

All Souls
See the future;
For the future is death,
Omnipresent with life and as
Awful.

Footnote: The poem consists of four cinquains in 2-4-6-8-2 syllabic form, each one expressing an idea about the major Christian festivals. 'Awful' is used in its true sense of 'inspiring awe', worthy of profound respect.

SCHOOL

A place of learning
Canned knowledge
Stuffed down your throat
Only to be spewed up
For exams and then forgotten.

A place of disciplining
The mind and body,
Having rules without the rod,
Where you can play up
And get out of anything.

A place of working
With irrelevant facts
And pointless information,
Killing interest and
Promoting boredom and ignorance.

A place of teaching
The end, not the beginning,
Of learning about
The unexplored boundaries
Of the world and oneself.

A place of thinking,
Where you are conditioned
To give the right answers
To all the wrong questions
About why you go to school.

*Footnote: Written while invigilating a GCSE examination
in the school hall at Axminster.*

THE ARTIST AND THE MIRROR

The artist deals in what is truth and what is not.
He shows us what he can of life
By hanging up a mirror on the wall.
The glass, sometimes distorted, does not change.
People look and read and listen;
Gleaning what they may from what
Is spoken, seen or sung or written.

The artist is a teacher and he teaches what is real,
Reflecting life in all it's many forms
By hanging up a mirror on the wall.
The wall revolves and images appear.
People look and read and listen
Hoping they can see themselves in what
Is spoken, seen or sung or written.

The artist observes the world in which he lives
Creating new impressions for the inner eye
By hanging up a mirror on the wall.
The framework varies in size and depth.
People look and read and listen
Drawing false conclusions from what
Is spoken, seen or sung or written.

The artist, inspired by generosity and love,
Offers help to those who want to live
By hanging up a mirror on the wall.
He projects himself unwillingly, though
People look and read and listen,
Believing they can share his life from what
Is spoken, seen or sung or written.

The artist is a man apart, destined to suffer
The indignities of a martyr
By hanging up a mirror on the wall.
He gives himself to his calling, while
People look and read and listen
Knowing not the meaning nor the mysteries in what
Is spoken, seen or sung or written.

The artist proclaims his message to the world
Communicating all he possibly can,
By hanging up a mirror on the wall.
He hates the artificial, unoriginal or false, but
People look and read and listen
Passing superficial judgements on what
Is spoken, seen or sung or written.

THE KNOCK UPON YOUR DOOR

As you sit and ponder in your
Semi-detached suburban home,
Do you ever wonder why
You live at all?

Washing the dishes, cleaning the floor,
Darning and mending,
Do you stop
To answer the knock upon your door?

As you relax in your favourite chair,
Head back and cool,
Do you ever wonder why
You live at all?

Watching the tele, reading a book,
Hoping and praying,
Do you rise
To answer the knock upon your door?

As you take off your clothes
And prepare for bed,
Do you ever wonder why
You live at all?

Making a meal, checking your change,
Scrimping and saving,
Do you run
To answer the knock upon your door?

As you lay awake beneath the sheets,
Your body limp,
Do you ever wonder why
You live at all?

Feeding your child, wiping the tears,
Caring and tending,
Do you need
To answer the knock upon your door?

As you eat your breakfast
In the early morn
Do you ever wonder why
You live at all?

Cleaning your shoes, leaving the house,
Rushing and cursing:
Do you remember
The sound of knocking on your door?

No one is there.
Your lover in despair has gone
And you were the one
Who ignored
His knocking on your door.
His heart is cold
His love is dead.
And you,
Who walk along the street
All dressed to kill,
Do you ever wonder why
You live at all?

TO THE NATIONAL HEALTH: 2040

On Eurotel channel 12 tonight
A documentary showed the plight
Of the Mid Century medical Service.
The Polyblow-structured hospitals
With inflatable research tentacles
Are fast becoming obsolescent buildings.
Body-monitoring cannot be maintained
Due to lack of staff and fiscal difficulties.
Investment in low cost systems stays the same
And preventative medicine will continue
With Repair Banks phased out gradually
Now that people are free
From physical impairment
And deformity.

Delayed conception for the nation
With its teenage sterilisation
Will no longer be compulsory.
Married couples will be permitted,
If proven genetically suited,
To procreate - no more than two children,
If they can pay the Reproduction Tax!
Families with defects are, of course, excluded.
Check your medico-history for the facts.
Free chromosome analysis
And genetic prognosis on DVD,
Computerised for all to see,
Any abnormalities
There happen to be.

Then reversible sterilisation
May be obtained by consultation
With a doctor at the local surgery.
Advice by law and licence granted,
Options of donor cells are offered;
Choice of method, colour, eyes and sex.
The cost is loss of individual privacy.
Tax credits for breast feeding was mentioned next.
For children there will be sugarless sweets
And lollies with fluoride centres to stop decay!
With the latest micro-surgery
Transplants of the kidneys
Using goats, medically
Prepared, are easy.

The plague - the motor car - is finished,
Thanks to the 'Ways of Walking' clinics.
Bicycles and tricycles are commended.
The tasteless soya bean supplement
To our annual meat ration is now
In the range of 'Fibrol 51' foodstuffs.
The shops stock 'Big Tom' new hybrid tomatoes.
Relax with 'Euphori-Q' tranquillisers at home.
Attend the Lister Aseptic Fashion Shows.
Feed your folks Ambrosia, the elixir of youth.
All such slogans of advertisers sell
Products to keep us well.
Radiation treatment cures
Most physical ills.

Schizophrenia, in mental health,
Has been conquered like leukaemia;
Bio-chemical imbalances rectified,
While the rate of suicide increases.
The new Cerebral Activators
For the elderly can stem senility.
The Geriatric Stimulation Centres,
To be renovated for the over-eighties
Will run a new game called "Incontinences".
Life expectancy today is ninety-three years.
Ill health could become the poet's muse
To change the attitudes
Next century of students
In medical schools.

Footnote: *Written after watching a television programme on what the NHS might be like by the year 2040 AD, it took me 9 hours to write, starting in the morning and finishing in the evening of the same day. The poem actually consists of 5 stanzas of 14 lines of 9-9-11-9-9-11-11-12-11-12-9-6-7-5 syllables each.*

TREE SPEECH

The dawn chorus is
A natural alarm clock
Of signs and signals.

The sound messages
Are the battle cries of birds
In choral warfare.

Communication
System with a limited
Vocabulary.

Reports about food,
Boundaries and moods, to mates
Waiting in the wings.

Each species' mating
Call, is a sound barrier
To inter-breeding.

Be not deluded,
Even by the twitter and
Charm of chaffinches.

The birds sing to birds
While we talk to cats, which oft
Regard us as trees.

WHEN YOU ARE GONE

When you are gone
It will be like the setting of the sun.
Time will stand still
And the days will be empty
And difficult to fill.
The heart strings, like cat gut, will be cut.
No love songs to play,
Only memories of melodies
And chords of harmony now passed away.

When you are gone
My world will be shattered like a broken vase.
Sounds will be silent
And sights will be blurred.
The tears will well up
And choke in my throat, gripped in grief.
Little things forgotten,
Brought to mind, remembered;
Sentiments of pity, pain and passion, once begotten.

When you are gone
Your kindness and consideration will be lost.
The sure protection
Which you freely gave
Will remain a debt
Impossible to repay this side of death.
Did you ever know
When your eyes kissed mine
How little time we had before you had to go?

When you are gone
I shall miss your quiet words and ways;
Your inner peace
Which gave me confidence;
Your tender touch
Which cared and calmed my troubled breast.
Your love will live on,
Like the warmth of the sun,
In me and mine, when you are gone.

A FEW REVIEWS

About <u>Stepping Stones</u>

"The depth of these poems shows that they are the brainchild of an artist. The reader is in for a pleasant surprise, for the poems are not only for those who are very deep in literature but also for the layman. I find in him a subtlety that is hard to come across within the scope of modern poets." Jagdish Bhatt, Editor of Current Events, India's National Journal on World Affairs Vol 22 No. 10 November 1976.

"I like the poems immensely and have read through the book many times with increasing pleasure and enjoyment." GNG Smith MA, Vice Principal, Bede College, University of Durham, December 1975.

About <u>Reflecting In The Sun</u>

"I greatly enjoyed reading the poems for their clarity and directness. Once again, the poems really communicate." Charles Causley D. Lit, the Cornish poet and schoolteacher, November 1976

"Powerful and consistent, some effective if chilling poems." The Countryman.

About <u>Of Faith And Fortune</u>

"His enquiring mind travels over a variety of interests. He has a keen observant eye and sees life with a certain humour though he is deeply conscious of its pathos and tragedy." Muriel Hilton, The Inquirer, 14th January 1978

About <u>O Didaskalos</u>

"The varied subject matter of this enjoyable collection makes it a useful book for teachers looking for a teaching guide." Frank Clarke, The Teacher, November 1997.

"The title means 'Teacher' in New Testament Greek which seems appropriate to this collection of poems with its diversity of themes, forms and styles of rhyming and non-rhyming verse, thus making it suitable for use as a teaching guide for students of the art." Ken Ellison, New Hope International Review Vol 20, 1998 (By 2020 the book was on the reading list of a number of American Universities).

"Like any good teacher he challenges the reader/pupil to think for him/herself." Felicia Houssein, Christian Poetry Review No. 7, July 1997.

About <u>Collected Poems</u>

"The poet has combined a series of styles and topics throughout his life, thoughts and experiences. After a serious knee injury that was to stop him from playing sport… a new poet was born and published in anthologies, magazines and newspapers. A very well published volume." Dandelion Arts Magazine, London, March 2016.

"Highly enjoyable to anyone who is a devotee of poetry but also beneficial to those who are not much acquainted with this limb of the arts. The final poem is an emotional one concerning how to face death, entitled 'Last Orders' which would serve as a memorial for almost anyone." Coaching News, London Football Coaches Association, July 2015.

About <u>Selected Poems</u>

"I'm very attracted by the clarity and precision as well as the very proper density of thought. Cook's work sits comfortably within the Causley tradition: generous of spirit, uncomplicated and accessible. Familiar forms and occasional archaic syntax are supported by some approaches to rhymes and metre that are traditional and some which are more variable." Pulsar Poetry Webzine, September 2018.

ACKNOWLEDGEMENTS

I will be forever indebted to the following people for their help and encouragement in my early years of writing; the late George N. G. Smith MA, Vice Principal of The College Of The Venerable Bede, Durham University in the 1960s; the late Howard Sergeant MBE (for services to literature), promoter and publisher in the 1970s and the late Dr. Charles Causley, poet and teacher in the 1980s.

In more recent times I am extremely grateful to all those who have posted such positive reviews on the internet, especially Patrick Martin for his advice and many words of wisdom along the way.

Finally, I wish to thank Gail Tomkins and her team at Virtual Admin UK for self-publishing The Diamond Collection on my behalf. They have all been most diligent and helpful in producing such a "final curtain" to my poetic endeavours. A heartfelt "Thank You" to one and all.

M. J. Cook

CATALOGUE

Books in which the poems were first published:

STEPPING STONES (1975)

1   Colour
2   Colour Television
3   Crying
4   Drifting Away
5   Earth, Water, Fire And Air
6   Education
7   Friends
8   Knitting
9   Living Fantasy
10 Love
11 Mind
12 Mistakes
13 No Need For Salvation
14 Perspective
15 Questions About Life
16 Sacred Mushroom
17 School
18 School Cat
19 The Artist And The Mirror
20 The End Of Pride
21 The Four Seasons
22 The Knock Upon Your Door
23 The Potter
24 The Valley Of The Living Dead
25 Time
26 United
27 When You Are Gone
28 Where Were You?

REFLECTING IN THE SUN (1976)

OF FAITH AND FORTUNE (1977)

O DIDASKALOS (1997)

COLLECTED POEMS (2015)

THE DIAMOND COLLECTION (2022)

"A vinculo matrimonii"
(Latin meaning "from the bond of matrimony.")

Printed in Great Britain
by Amazon

81022014R00132